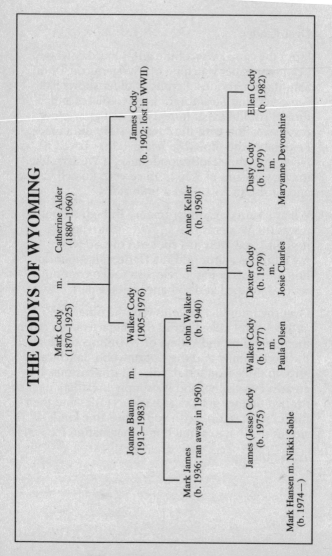

THE CODYS OF WYOMING

Mark Cody (1870–1925) m. Catherine Alder (1880–1960)

Joanne Baum (1913–1983) m.

James Cody (b. 1902; lost in WWII)

Walker Cody (1905–1976)

Mark James (b. 1936; ran away in 1950)

John Walker (b. 1940) m. Anne Keller (b. 1950)

James (Jesse) Cody (b. 1975)

Walker Cody (b. 1977) m. Paula Olsen

Dexter Cody (b. 1979) m. Josie Charles

Dusty Cody (b. 1979) m. Maryanne Devonshire

Ellen Cody (b. 1982)

Mark Hansen m. Nikki Sable (b. 1974—)

Dear Reader,

From the time I was a little girl, I loved cowboys. I can remember watching old Westerns on TV on Saturday afternoons. Reruns of older shows like *Gunsmoke* and *Bonanza* took me to places and times I couldn't visit in real life. As I grew older, my fascination with the cowboy story didn't fade. Remember the show *The Young Riders?* Loved it! Now every time Hollywood makes a Western like the new version of *3:10 to Yuma* with Russell Crowe and Christian Bale, I get a little giddy.

When I started reading romance in high school, it was the Westerns that I loved most. The romanticized West just spoke to me. So when my fabulous editor told me Harlequin American Romance was going to release a rodeo continuity series, I jumped at the chance to take part.

Over the months that followed, the other five authors and I talked about the characters, the ranch, the mountains and valleys of Wyoming. Gradually the Cody family and the Cottonwood Ranch came alive in three wonderful, colorful dimensions. It's an area I've visited, and it's simply breathtaking. I'm thrilled that we get to share these stories and their magnificent setting with you—the same kinds of stories that have captured my imagination for years.

Trish Milburn

Elly: Cowgirl Bride
TRISH MILBURN

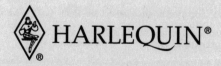

HARLEQUIN®

TORONTO • NEW YORK • LONDON
AMSTERDAM • PARIS • SYDNEY • HAMBURG
STOCKHOLM • ATHENS • TOKYO • MILAN • MADRID
PRAGUE • WARSAW • BUDAPEST • AUCKLAND

Recycling programs
for this product may
not exist in your area.

ISBN-13: 978-0-373-75330-7

ELLY: COWGIRL BRIDE

Copyright © 2010 by Trish Milburn

ABOUT THE AUTHOR

Trish Milburn wrote her first book in the fifth grade and has the cardboard-and-fabric-bound, handwritten and colored-pencil-illustrated copy to prove it. That "book" was called *Land of the Misty Gems*, and not surprisingly it was a romance. She's always loved stories with happy endings, whether those stories come in the form of books, movies, TV programs or marriage to her own hero.

A print journalist by trade, she still does contract and freelance work in that field, balancing those duties with her dream-come-true career as a novelist. Before she published her first book, she was a finalist eight times in the prestigious Golden Heart contest sponsored by Romance Writers of America, winning twice. Other than reading, Trish enjoys traveling (by car or train—she's a terra firma girl!), watching TV and movies, hiking, nature photography and visiting national parks.

You can visit Trish online at www.trishmilburn.com. Readers also can write to her at P.O. Box 140875, Nashville, TN 37214-0875.

Books by Trish Milburn

HARLEQUIN AMERICAN ROMANCE

To all those writers—of books, TV shows and movies—who made the West and the people who call it home come alive in your stories.

As always, to Shane for being supportive and loving.

And to my wonderful career partners— my agent, Michelle Grajkowski, and my editor, Johanna Raisanen. I think we make a fantastic trio.

Chapter One

Elly inhaled the crisp morning air, felt it warm as it flowed into her lungs. Nothing better than a ride on a clear November morning to make her feel alive. She pulled her horse, Pepper, to a halt at the top of a ridge beyond the Cottonwood Ranch's homestead.

"Surveying your domain, Princess Cody?" asked her best friend, Janie Hansen, as she stopped beside Elly.

Elly thought she heard an edge of some unfamiliar emotion—resentment?—in Janie's voice. But when she turned and saw no visible evidence on Janie's face, she dismissed it as a product of less-than-restful sleep the night before. The race to the National Finals Rodeo was beginning to stress her out.

Elly laughed. "Yeah, I'm already plotting my takeover of the rest of Wyoming." She steepled her fingers and squinted as if devising an evil plan of domination.

The fact was that everything within her view, with the exception of the far peaks of the Rockies to the west, was Cody land, had been for years even before her birth. The Cottonwood was home to snowcapped mountains, lush valleys, waterways of various sizes, and seemingly endless stretches of rangeland dotted with cattle, horses and natural gas wells.

She loved it all, every square foot, but adding to the substantial acreage wasn't at the top of her to-do list. Winning the national barrel-racing championship was firmly entrenched in that spot. She wanted to make it to the NFR in Las Vegas so much that lately she'd been having odd dreams about competing on a course set up in the middle of a glitzy casino while showgirls cheered off to the sides.

"Well, let me know when you're amassing your minions," Janie said as she urged Chica, her palomino, into a slow walk. "I'm always in the market for more work."

Even after all the years they'd known each other, Elly experienced a pang of guilt that she'd been born into wealth while Janie…well, hadn't. But she didn't show how she felt because Janie was nothing if not proud. Besides, Janie was a hard worker and good at saving her money—with an occasional splurge.

Elly wondered sometimes if Janie let herself make those splurges only to keep her sanity in a never-ending cycle of work. Just thinking about the hours Janie put in working at the Feed and Grain, helping Dr. Bill with his vet practice, studying for her veterinary classes, riding in rodeo competitions and caring for her mother made Elly marvel that her friend even stayed upright.

Elly urged Pepper to keep pace with Chica. "So, we're due for a girls' weekend. Any ideas where you want to go?"

They tossed out ideas—a spa day in Jackson, window-shopping and dinner in Casper, a movie marathon complete with all the junk food they could consume— during the rest of their trip back down to the barn. But something about Janie's halfhearted contributions to the discussion worried Elly.

"Is something wrong?"

It took Janie a moment to shake her head. "Just tired."

The breeze kicked up as they dismounted. "Have to say a trip to Miami is sounding good to me right now," Janie said as she flipped up the lamb's-wool collar on her denim jacket.

"I'll check on airfares this afternoon," Elly joked as she led Pepper to the open doorway of the barn, even though she knew Janie couldn't afford to part with the money or the time away from home. "Want to come in for some coffee?"

"Sounds good, but I've got to get going." Janie opened the back of her aging horse trailer with a screech of metal and guided Chica inside. "Got to get to work an hour earlier than normal. Ruth's got to take Leslie to a doctor's appointment in Sheridan."

Ruth and Leslie Pearsoll owned the Markton Feed and Grain, where Janie had worked since she was sixteen.

"He okay?"

Janie laughed, sounding more like herself. "He says it's just 'routine maintenance' like for anything that has a lot of miles on it." Her affection for her employer was apparent in her amused smile.

The Pearsolls had always treated Janie as if she were their own daughter, especially after their son, Troy, had been killed in a rodeo accident six years ago. And with an alcoholic father and a mom slowly descending into dementia, Janie had needed the Pearsolls as much more than employers. The Pearsolls were good people who judged others on their own merits, not on the size of their bank accounts. The same couldn't be said of all of Markton's residents.

Janie closed and latched the trailer, then shivered when a gust of wind buffeted her and rattled the metal of the trailer's sides. "Yep, the beach definitely sounds good. Talk to you later."

Elly waved as she led Pepper into the barn to feed and groom her. She smoothed her hand along Pepper's sleek, black neck. "Don't worry, girl. Hopefully, next month we'll both get a little warm weather."

In Las Vegas, home to the National Finals Rodeo. The finish line for a dream Elly had been chasing around barrels for years.

"I'll give you a bit of rest, girl, but we're practicing hard this afternoon."

While Pepper enjoyed a little downtime, Elly had work to do. Every member of the Cody family had some aspect of the ranch to run, and her contribution as PR guru demanded time in front of the computer—answering e-mails, updating the ranch's Web site and posting daily entries on the Cottonwood Chronicles blog. The blog had made her friends around the world and garnered her media coverage for the ranch and its diversified businesses. She was the go-to girl for booking tours of the ranch, too.

She beat clumps of frosty mud off her scuffed boots before stepping up onto the front porch of the old homestead house she shared with her oldest brother, Jesse. The way her brothers had been finding love and moving out lately, she wondered if she might have the place all to herself soon. Lately, that had been more appealing. Ever since Jesse's good friend Nicki Sable had married Mark Hansen, his chief bull-riding rival, Jesse had been in a nasty mood.

Despite the way Cupid was finding his way around the ranch, it was hard to imagine Jesse taking a break from work long enough to hook up with anyone. Sometimes she wondered if he still mourned Laurie, his last serious girlfriend, whom he'd lost to cancer. Laurie had been great, but Jesse needed to move on at some point.

Thinking she'd have a couple of hours of quiet to work on Web site updates, Elly was surprised to hear voices coming from the small office when she stepped inside the front door. She hung her jacket on the coat tree in the corner and walked toward the sounds of conversation.

Jesse normally conducted ranch business at the ranch's official office in the converted bunkhouse, so she was surprised to see a man in a suit sitting opposite him. She paused outside the open door, drawing her brother's attention. He stiffened and glanced back at his guest just as the man turned to face her.

Visitors came and went every day, but it'd been a long time—maybe never—since someone that good-looking had set foot on the Cottonwood. Both men stood, allowing her to more fully appreciate the stranger's height, light brown hair and eyes so dark that they reminded her of some luscious chocolates an online friend had sent her from Paris.

"Elly, I thought you were out riding with Janie," Jesse said. He sounded like he wished she still were. It took a moment for that realization to sink in because Elly suddenly had a hard time focusing on anything besides the stranger in the room.

She mentally shook herself, then managed to form words quickly enough that she didn't appear as if she'd taken too many hooves to the head. "I was. We both had work, though."

Elly forced herself to look at Jesse, whose glances back and forth between her and the other man made her brother look oddly uncomfortable. What the heck was going on?

He exhaled and nodded at the visitor. "You remember Will Jackson."

Will Jackson? She looked back at the man and saw nothing of the kid she used to know before he and his gigantic brain had gone off to college when he was sixteen. But when he smiled, something about the shape of it and the crinkle around his eyes revealed a spark of the boy she and Janie used to call Billy the Kid. Damn, but Billy the Kid Jackson had grown up to be Droolworthy-Hot Jackson.

A little laugh escaped her. "Will, huh? I wouldn't have known you if I'd passed you on the street."

"And you look exactly the same." Was that a note of appreciation in his voice or her neglected libido's imagination?

He extended his hand, and she took it. Firm, and with some surprising calluses for a man in a suit. She liked that. She fought the urge to give him a hug. Never had she been jittery or awkward around him when they'd been younger, but both of those feelings assaulted her now. He was the same person, right? Just sexier. Janie was going to swallow her tongue when she saw him.

He kept the handshake brief, as if he wanted to keep physical contact to a minimum.

"So, what brings you out here?" And why was he dressed in a spiffy, charcoal-gray suit complete with ice blue tie?

A look passed between Will and Jesse, one she couldn't quite pin down. Secretive, maybe.

Jesse rounded his desk. "Thanks for coming by, Will. I'll be in touch." He seemed way too eager to get Will away from her, and she doubted it was part of his and her other three brothers' ongoing efforts to keep her safe from anyone with a Y chromosome. The Cody gauntlet of Jesse, Walker, Dex and Dusty.

"What's going on, Jesse?"

"Nothing."

Elly rolled her eyes. Twenty-five years he'd known her, and still he hadn't figured out that she could always tell when he was lying. But those years had also taught her that once he made up his mind not to say something, it took drastic measures to loosen his tongue.

She took a step forward, placing herself between Will and Jesse but facing Will. "Why all the mystery?"

Some of Will's new look of confidence slipped at her question, and she saw a hint of the unsure boy he used to be—even though she had to look up at him now.

Jesse sighed heavily behind her. "Will's an attorney now. I hired him."

Elly held Will's dark gaze for a moment more before leaning back on the front of the desk and facing her brother. "Something going on with the drilling operation?"

"No."

When Jesse didn't elaborate and she noticed the tight way he held his jaw, a kernel of concern formed in her stomach. "What's wrong?"

Jesse ran his hand through his hair. "You have to keep this quiet. You can't breathe a word to Mom or Dad."

"Jesse," she said more firmly.

A wave of fatigue seemed to descend on him, causing his shoulders to slump. He made his way back to his big, leather desk chair and sank into it.

Elly turned to face him again, but she didn't sit. Instead, she crossed her arms and waited for an answer.

Jesse stared at nothing for a few seconds before meeting her eyes. "Mark Hansen may be Dad's son."

"What?" She stared at him, thinking she'd surely misheard. His words made absolutely no sense—despite murmured rumors throughout the years. "That's ridiculous."

"I've hired Will to look into how it could affect the family should Mark make a paternity claim."

"Why? It's not true. Where did you get this crazy idea?"

"He didn't deny it."

"Who?"

"Dad," Jesse said, his voice strained.

Elly dropped into the leather chair behind her, shock robbing her of the strength to stand. "I don't understand."

Will reclaimed his seat in the other guest chair. "We don't have incontrovertible proof. There are a lot of questions to be answered."

Elly let the words sink in but didn't look at Will. Instead, she held her brother's gaze. "I don't understand why I can't say anything to Mom and Dad. I want to know what's going on."

"Because they don't know that I've contacted Will, and they don't need to. It's my responsibility to make sure any and all threats to this family are dealt with."

"You sound like some sort of cowboy crime boss," she said.

"I'm not the bad guy here."

She didn't want to think of her father as a bad guy, either. Or Mark. He'd always been kind of like another older brother—kidding her, helping Janie and her out of scrapes, watching out for her welfare.

That thought stopped her. Even the idea that he

actually was her brother…no, she couldn't go there. Couldn't think about what that would mean her father had done. He was the ultimate family man, who put family and legacy before everything.

"Has Mark said anything?"

"No, not to me anyway."

"Then why is this an issue?"

"I have my reasons."

Elly redirected her attention to Will. "No offense to you, but this is a total waste of time and money."

He glanced at Jesse.

"It has to be done, Elly," Jesse said.

She shot him a frustrated look. "Why?"

"Because I overheard Mom and Dad talking, the morning of Nicki and Mark's wedding. At the very least, Dad had an affair with Abigail Hansen."

Elly shot out of her chair, circled behind it and gripped the back until her knuckles whitened. "This is insane." She couldn't even look at Will as anger and embarrassment heated her cheeks.

"The rumors have been around for years, but that's all I thought they were. I even threatened to punch more than one person I heard spreading them." He sighed, sounding as tired as if he'd been up for three days straight. "Lately, the rumors have increased. Then I heard… An affair did happen, and the timing leaves Mark's paternity in question."

"Did you ask Dad, point blank?"

"I confronted him. He refused to talk about it. Mom, too."

Her mouth parted in disbelief. "So you decided to go behind their backs?" she asked, her voice rising.

His expression hardened, and his eyes narrowed. "I'm getting to the bottom of things as quickly and quietly as possible. I'd rather be on offense than defense."

Everything sank into her brain like rain trickling through porous rock. She'd been aware of the vague whispers about her dad not being faithful, but she had never, ever thought they might be true. She'd always attributed them to people being jealous of the Cody fortune. They had angered her because every single member of the Cody family worked hard for what they had and helped others in more ways than she could count.

But was John Walker Cody an adulterer after all?

Tears stung her eyes. She had to get out of the too-small room, away from the idea that her father had broken his most sacred vow. She hated the idea that Will, someone outside the family, knew what might end up being the ugliest of all secrets.

"Goodbye, Will." She headed out the door before he or Jesse could say anything. Long, angry steps took her to her bedroom, where she grabbed her camera before turning to leave again.

Jesse stood in the open doorway. "Where are you going?"

"Out."

"Where?" he demanded.

She met his eyes. "For a ride, to clear my head." She shoved past him and out the back door so she wouldn't have to see Will again. The chill soaked through her shirtsleeves, but she wasn't about to go back inside for her coat. She'd grab one of the work jackets belonging to the hands. The cold was what she needed. Maybe the purity of the air, its bite, would help clear the awful images from her mind.

Once inside the dimmer confines of the barn, she stopped outside Pepper's stall and allowed the horse to nuzzle the top of her head as she leaned her forehead against the wooden door.

"Don't worry, girl. I won't interrupt your break."

Elly patted Pepper, then grabbed Slim's lined ranch coat as she moved down to where Jasmine was already saddled. She mounted and headed out into the bright sunshine, intent on finding beautiful images to capture. Beauty to block out the ugliness.

Her gaze found the newer, more elaborate house on a distant hill. What were her parents doing right now? Were they arguing, filling the large, open spaces of their dream house with their anger? Was her father regretting letting Jesse believe the preposterous claim by not denying it? Or was he out riding fence lines at the far reaches of the ranch, leaving her mom alone with the pain of betrayal?

She shuddered to think how her father would react if he found out Jesse had launched an investigation.

Why had Jesse done so? Did he not trust their parents to take care of the family? The ranch? Did he have a point? Did he fear losing his place as the eldest heir or having to share his inheritance with yet another person—one with whom he hadn't even grown up?

Or was this just him striking out against Mark because of their long-standing, and stupid, rivalry on the rodeo circuit? God, she couldn't even remember when it had started or why. Could they? She'd thought it was finally over when they'd shaken hands after the rodeo in Oklahoma, but that must have been too much to hope for.

Tears pooled when she thought of what this might do to her friendship with Janie. She absolutely could not lose her. Janie was more than a best friend. She was the sister Elly had never had.

But if it came down to picking sides, Janie would have to side with her brother, wouldn't she? Did Janie have any inkling that she and Mark might not have the same father?

So many questions pressed in on Elly that she felt she had to escape or howl. She pointed Jasmine to the west and urged the horse into a gallop. Maybe she could outrun everything threatening to make her world disintegrate around her.

WILL RESISTED THE POWERFUL desire to follow Elly outside, to somehow offer her comfort. At least an ear or shoulder. A friend.

Who was he kidding? He cursed himself for wanting to be near her. Her long, blond hair and blue-green eyes, the shape of her face made her even more beautiful now than she'd been as a teenager when she'd occupied way too many of his thoughts. Despite his seven years away from Markton, despite the fact that she was the cause of the biggest humiliation of his life, Ellen Anne Cody still made his heart beat triple time.

"Sorry about that," Jesse said as he walked back into the foyer outside the office.

"No need to apologize. Understandable that it was a shock."

Jesse glanced toward the back door, through which Elly had disappeared, before extending his hand. "Thanks for stopping by. I'd appreciate it if you kept everything quiet."

"I'll be discreet." A twinge of inferiority straight out of his past hit Will, a voice telling him that real men, men like the Codys, didn't use words like *discreet*. Only bookish nerds like him.

Only he was more than that now.

He gripped Jesse's hand in a firm handshake while berating himself for letting the old doubts surface. It was something about being here on the ranch, where he'd once longed to be like the cowboys who filled Elly's life. But he wasn't the boy he'd been at sixteen anymore. He no longer judged his worth based on what a Cody thought of him.

Was he now the type of man who could interest Elly Cody?

Not that he planned to find out anytime soon. She hadn't been interested before, so he told himself it didn't matter if she was now. Plus, now was not the time to investigate his chances with her, even if he wanted to.

Rather, he had to investigate whether she had yet another brother. Nothing like diving into the deep end with his new practice, representing one of the wealthiest and most powerful families in Wyoming.

He headed for his Yukon and stopped beside it when he noticed Elly riding away from the barn, her braid bouncing against her back. He sighed. One look—that was all it had taken for him to realize the years away and the memory of her killing his hope of being with her still hadn't managed to get Elly out of his system.

She was a disease, one for which he had to find a cure before he did something stupid like ask her out again. Maybe the passage of time would lend a hand. Elly might be seeing someone. Damn, she might even be married for all he knew. That thought made him sick to his stomach. Should he have returned to Wyoming sooner and not taken no for an answer a second time? Or should he have just stayed away and not chanced renewing old feelings?

Jesse stepped out onto the porch. Not wanting to get caught ogling the man's sister, Will opened the SUV's door and tossed his leather folder inside.

"I'll call as soon as I know something."

Jesse nodded. Will slid into the driver's seat and headed down the ranch's entrance road. His training kicked into gear as he started mentally mapping out the tasks before him. He eyed the elder Codys' house on its hilltop perch a couple of miles away. He'd first seen it in a magazine, not surprised it was a masterwork of stone, gleaming logs and glass. A testament to the wealth attached to the name Cody.

Though he'd never been close to J. W. Cody, he found himself wanting to make sure everything turned out as well as it could for him. Not for the man's sake, especially if he'd committed adultery and fathered a child with another woman, but for Elly's. Despite the lingering sting of that long-ago rejection, he didn't want to do anything that would hurt her unnecessarily. Rather, he wanted to do his job to help his client and hoped she respected that.

And if he was lucky, Elly would see him as someone other than that ridiculous Billy the Kid, a moniker that belonged to someone who didn't really exist anymore.

He was a mile or so down the highway that ran adjacent to the ranch's northern edge when he noticed movement on top of a ridge. He slowed, then pulled over to the side of the road.

Elly sat atop a gold-colored horse as she stared in his direction. At least he told himself she was looking at him. Even after all that she'd heard minutes before, was she as curious about the adult him as he was about the adult her?

Chapter Two

No matter which way she turned, Elly couldn't get comfortable. She tried going to sleep on her back, on her side, on her stomach. With the thick comforter on, with it tossed to the foot of the bed. Counting sheep didn't help. Neither did mentally going over her to-do list for the next day—all the tasks she had planned to tackle today but had abandoned after the news about her father and Mark.

She couldn't even call up Janie and talk, like she normally would when something was bothering her. Elly's parents weren't on the conversation list, and her brothers weren't exactly the "let's talk out our feelings" type of guys.

The image of Will Jackson filled her mind. The Will of today, not the young boy who'd worn gawky glasses and been allergic to just about every animal on the ranch. She realized he hadn't been wearing glasses earlier in the day. Nothing had obscured her view of his dark, beautiful eyes. Had he always possessed the type of eyes that drew a woman in? Had she just not noticed?

Elly closed her eyes and slowly went over what she remembered of Will's appearance when he'd stood to face her in the office. He'd been tanned, so he must spend time outdoors doing something. Though he'd been wearing a suit, he'd filled it out nicely without seeming to bust at the seams. The face of young Will had grown into a more masculine version of itself, making the angles of his jaws and planes of his cheeks much more attractive.

Yes, Will Jackson as an adult was as sexy as the summer nights were long. And that felt odd to admit.

Elly's skin heated, and she gave up any hope of sleeping. She swung around to sit on the side of the bed and wished her brain had an off switch. She shook her head and meandered out of her bedroom into the middle of the quiet house. She didn't know where Jesse was. Maybe instead of lying in bed sleepless, he was out knocking back a few to dull his thoughts.

TV wouldn't keep her attention, either, so she decided she might as well make productive use of her time and headed for the corner where a new supply of photo matting stood. She grabbed a couple of pieces and the rest of her tools and placed them on the dining room table.

Next, she chose two prints she wanted to mat and frame. If she could finish several of her framed prints—ones that captured the people, places and seasons of the Cottonwood Ranch—she'd make a trip into nearby Cody to deliver them to the gallery that sold her work.

She chose a shot of falling rain taken from inside the barn and another of her brothers on horseback silhouetted against a pink twilight sky. She ran her fingers over their images and wondered if it was possible there should be a fifth horseman in the photo instead of the four she'd known for all of her twenty-five years.

With a shake of her head, she got to work. As she was finishing the second framing job, the sound of Jesse's boots against the front porch brought her out of her meandering thoughts. She turned around in the dining room chair, curious just how inebriated her brother might be.

But he didn't act drunk as he came in the front door, slowly hung up his coat and trudged in her direction. No, he appeared more drained than anything. He looked five years older than he had a few days ago. Only then did she realize he'd been looking extra tired recently— ever since the rodeo in Oklahoma. There had been an awkward moment after the rodeo was over when he and Mark had shaken hands with the Cody clan watching. When her father had congratulated Mark on his win. It all held so much more significance now.

She'd figured he'd just been pushing himself too hard lately, as he was wont to do. After all, he had a lot of ranch responsibilities in addition to his bull-riding practice and travel to rodeos.

She felt bad for biting his head off earlier, for running out when she should have stayed to lend her support. But she still wasn't sure how she felt about him hiring Will behind her parents' backs. Yes, she understood his desire to protect the family, but it just felt…wrong somehow.

Which now made her wonder why Will had taken the job. He'd always seemed like a good guy. It'd be sad if law school had changed that about him.

Jesse sank into a chair at the end of the table without making eye contact. She didn't say a word as she rose and went to slice him a piece of the red velvet cake her mother had dropped off while they'd been away from the homestead.

Now that she thought about it, she realized her mom had been baking a lot over the past several days. The number of desserts floating around the ranch should have been the first, calorie-laden clue that something was wrong. Everyone in her family had some unique way of dealing with stress. Anne Cody's was to bake—a lot.

Evidently, she'd formed the habit early in her marriage when she'd had a breakdown after miscarrying her first child. Nobody talked about that fragile time, and over the years the baking had just become a normal stress reliever, nothing to cause the rest of the family to watch her closely.

Unless she was baking enough to open her own bakery.

As Elly slid the hefty piece of cake onto a saucer, she now attached new meaning to her father's absence from the main part of the ranch the past couple of days. Normally, employees rode the fence lines, but she hadn't thought much about it when her dad had done so. Sometimes he still liked to get out and ride the far reaches of the Cottonwood to be alone with his thoughts. Maybe this time, he'd gone to reflect on his mistakes.

Elly placed the cake and a glass of milk in front of Jesse and returned to her own seat.

"Thanks," he said, sounding as tired as he looked.

So many questions begged to be voiced, but she didn't know how to start a conversation about the torpedo that had slammed into their lives. But the silence pressed in on her more than the dread of what Jesse might say.

"What made you hire Will?"

She hadn't expected that to be the question to come out of her mouth. But it wasn't really a surprise when she considered how much she'd been thinking about him earlier, how curious she was about where he'd been, what he'd done since he'd left Markton. And why he was back in the area.

Jesse sighed. "I told you. I need to see how this could affect all of us and the ranch if it's true and it comes to light."

Elly shook her head. "No, I know that. I meant, why Will instead of another lawyer? He must only barely be out of law school."

"He was familiar with the ranch, with our family. Had always seemed like a friend."

"And it didn't bother you that you were revealing this ugly secret to someone who knows us?"

Jesse set down the fork he'd just picked up. "Of course, it did. But it was better than the idea of laying it all out for some outsider." He tapped the tines of the fork against the edge of the saucer. "And Dad might have admitted to the affair, but I want proof of Mark's paternity before I believe it."

"If Mark were to make such a claim, why would he lie about it?"

"I don't know. Money maybe."

Elly stared at Jesse, wondering where the bitter person in front of her had come from. "You've known Mark your entire life. I know you have some sort of stupid testosterone rivalry thing dating back to before either of you had to shave, but the idea of him lying to get his hands on our money is just ludicrous. And you know it."

Jesse shoved the cake away. "I don't know what to think. Do you?"

She let out a breath before shaking her head. "No." She glanced around the kitchen where she and her brothers had grown up. "God, how are we supposed to act around Mom and Dad?"

"Like we always do."

"I don't think that's possible."

"It has to be, at least until they say something to you or I figure out what this all means for us."

How was she going to look at her mother without pity in her eyes? At her dad without anger and resentment?

"Elly?"

"Fine."

Elly stared at Jesse. "Do you think Mark even knows?"

Jesse shook his head a couple of times. "Don't know.

One of the things we'll need to find out if it turns out to be true."

With an exhale that spoke of a fatigue for the ages, Jesse rose from the table and headed for his room. Elly didn't attempt to stop him or pull him deeper into conversation. She doubted he could shed light on her foremost question anyway—why would her father cheat on her mother when they'd had a long, happy marriage since? At least she'd always thought they had.

Elly grabbed the abandoned slice of cake and shoved a giant bite in her mouth. Her mother baked when she was upset, and Elly consumed the results when she found herself in a similar state. She had to force herself not to bite down too hard on the fork when a second bite followed the first in a vain effort to make her feel better.

If the situation wasn't resolved soon, she was going to end up the size of Wyoming.

WILL REVIEWED THE NOTES he'd made about the Cody case then sat back in his office chair. How ironic that one of his first cases after moving back to the area involved Elly's family. He closed his eyes and thought back to the moment he'd seen her the day before, more beautiful than even his vivid memories had prepared him for. He hadn't been able to get her out of his mind since their gazes had connected.

But being with her was no more realistic now than when he'd been a geeky, allergy-ridden teen. Only this time it was his work that stood in the way—not the fact that she wouldn't look at him as anything other than a casual friend. And there was his pride. And the promise he'd made to himself on the heels of her rejection to never let himself get that attached ever again. Besides, the current situation with her parents likely didn't foster romantic notions in her mind. He tried to imagine how she must feel, how he would have felt if he'd ever found out his dad had cheated on his mom.

He couldn't help that part of him wished he'd bumped into Elly under different circumstances. He now knew that Elly wasn't married. Delia Barstow, his secretary, had filled him in with a lot of details. Elly and Jesse were the only two unattached Cody siblings, and word was neither of them was seeing anyone.

It had taken a monumental effort not to react with excited possibility when Delia had imparted the news about Elly.

Damn, he was pitiful. Still stuck on the same girl he'd fantasized about since he'd developed hormones. The one who'd actually laughed when he'd offered to take her to prom.

He glanced at the clock and decided to take a break to pick up some lunch and look for a birthday present for his mom. Maybe getting outside and walking would help him settle on his next move in the case and stop thinking about Elly.

"Delia, I'm headed out for bit."

"Okay."

"Need anything while I'm out?"

"A winning lotto ticket and a good man would be fab, if you can swing it."

Will laughed. "I'll see what I can do."

He was still smiling when he reached the sidewalk that led into the downtown area of Cody. Delia was as funny now as she'd been when they'd gone to high school together. That was part of why he'd hired her, to ease his clients' anxiety.

Plus, they worked well together. Mrs. Threadmiller's biology lab had proven that when they'd been lab partners. If you got out of that class without murdering your lab partner, that was a very good sign it was a working match made in heaven.

Another bonus was that she hadn't demanded a huge salary. And just starting out, without a lot of experience to recommend him, he needed to watch his bottom line until he saw how things would shake out. Especially when he was trying to make a go of it in a small town where the other attorneys had been there since he was a toddler.

He slowed when he reached the line of shops showcasing gift options in their front windows—everything from T-shirts to high-end artwork. At the Tangled Antlers Gallery, he noticed a painting of the area's red-rock cliffs he thought his mom might like. Movement inside the store caught his attention, and he glanced up. Elly stood talking to another woman. He blinked, wondering if his imagination had gone three-dimensional. But no, she was still there when his eyes reopened.

Curious what had brought her to Cody, he headed

for the door. Damned if he didn't wish that he was the reason for her visit to Markton's bigger neighbor, but her current location said otherwise. Still, he couldn't pass up the opportunity to say hello, to stand near her again, maybe even have a chance to catch up a little without Jesse's large presence looming. He could allow himself to be around her without making a fool of himself or getting in too deep, right?

"I'll be with you in a moment," the woman talking to Elly said when she spotted him.

Elly glanced his way. "Will." Surprise filled her voice and widened her eyes.

He couldn't tell for sure, but he thought her cheeks pinkened in embarrassment. Great, he was going to be forever associated with her father's infidelity. Not exactly what he'd been going for when he'd walked through the gallery's door. But he was inside now, and he couldn't just leave without making the situation even more embarrassing for both of them.

"Doing a little shopping?" he asked.

"Uh, no."

The older woman brightened. "Elly is quite the talented photographer. And she's just dropped off some of her newest work." She spun a large, framed photo around to show him. The scene was of a mother duck leading her brood out onto bright green grass. The captured moment was so lifelike. He imagined he could hear the little quacks of the ducklings and smell the damp scent of early morning depicted by the dew on the grass leaves.

"That's really good."

The gallery lady, perhaps smelling a sale, directed him toward a corner where several framed prints hung on the adjacent walls. A larger one sat displayed on an easel. As he moved closer, he noticed the bigger piece was of a giant bull moose chomping on his latest meal as he stood in the shallows of a stream.

On a rectangular sign hanging from the ceiling above the display, a stylized script read, "The Cottonwood Collection, One-of-a-Kind Prints by Ellen Cody."

"I'm impressed," he said as he turned to meet Elly's eyes.

She shrugged like this accomplishment was no big deal. He remembered how she'd always had one of those point-and-shoot cameras, clicking off photos constantly, when they were kids. But he had no idea she'd harbored this kind of talent.

Why did she look so uncomfortable? Was she afraid he'd say something about the case? She should know he couldn't, and would never, do that. Or was her discomfort because of her photos? He couldn't imagine why.

Her images showed a love of the land, and the people and animals who populated it. Something about them made him wonder if Elly was as different from her teenage self as he was.

He returned his attention to the photograph of the moose. It really was a fantastic shot, and he'd say that even if he hadn't once been halfway in love with the photographer. He pointed to it.

"If I buy this, will you autograph it?"

"Will," she said, sounding surprised he'd even consider it. "You don't have to do that."

He laughed. "I know I don't have to. I want to. It's for my mom, for her birthday. She has a fascination with moose. She'll love this. Even more so since you took it."

Will didn't take his gaze away from her until she nodded. Then he faced the other woman, who he'd gathered was named Stella and was the gallery's owner. "I'll take it. And can you gift wrap it for me for pickup later today?"

"Certainly."

When Stella lifted the framed photo from its easel and headed toward a large worktable in the middle of the gallery, Will hung back with Elly.

"I hope your mom likes it," she said.

"She will." He watched Elly, decided to let go of that past humiliation, chose to believe she hadn't meant to hurt him. That she probably didn't even remember it. Despite that one event, he knew in his heart she was a good person, someone he could be friends with again. "You know what else Mom would like?"

She met his eyes, and for a moment he was in danger of losing his ability to speak. He had to get past those types of reactions. He recovered just in time to prevent looking like an idiot.

"If you'd join us for her birthday dinner tonight. I'm taking her and Aunt Judith out."

Elly shook her head, sending her long, blond ponytail

waving gently back and forth. "I don't want to intrude on your family time."

"It's not intruding if I invited you." He smiled because just being around her made it impossible not to.

"But it's a family occasion. You haven't been back that long. I'm sure your mom wants to spend time with you."

"Oh, I plan to be there, too."

An unexpected laugh shot out of her.

"My mom always liked you. She'll be thrilled if you join us."

Not to mention how he'd feel. What was it about her, this one woman, that made his heart rate accelerate at the mere glimpse of her? He'd dated other beautiful women. Kate Sturgeon had even gotten her father to offer him a position in his law firm so he'd stay in Denver. But none of them had frazzled and thrilled and scared him like Elly did. Weren't you supposed to have a first crush then get over it?

But it hadn't been a simple crush, had it? Despite his young age, it had been true love for him. And evidently time hadn't seen fit to erase those feelings. He might be a fool for thinking they could just be friends, but that wasn't going to stop him from trying. If he was lucky, time with her would cause the old feelings to fade. Maybe all he'd want to be was friends.

Elly met his gaze again, gave him a considering look, then nodded. "Okay, sounds like fun. I haven't seen your mom in a while. I stay so busy, I barely see myself."

"Sounds like you need a night off then."

She pondered the thought for a moment, and he saw a hint of darkness pass over her features.

"You know, I think you're right," she finally said.

They fell back on aimless small talk as he paid for the photograph and Elly signed it with a gold marker in one corner. When she blew on the wet ink, a shiver of longing went over him. Man, he needed to get a grip. He wasn't a young, lovesick puppy anymore.

No, he was a grown man with a grown man's desires. And for some reason they all pushed him toward Elly. He'd done his best the past several years to avoid any mention of her, had even avoided rodeo coverage in the news because he knew he'd see her name, maybe even her picture. He'd wanted to get over her, hadn't wanted to torture himself with what he'd believed would never be.

"You okay?" Elly asked, startling him.

"Uh, yeah. So, we're meeting at the Bluff Steakhouse at seven."

"Sounds good. I'll see you then." She gave the marker back to Stella. "For now, I've got about a dozen more things on my to-do list." She glanced at the print. "I'm glad that one's going to someone I know. I had to sit still until I lost feeling in my legs to get that shot."

"It was worth it." He fought the urge to buy his mom another gift and keep the moose print for himself. As if he wasn't going to be thinking about Elly night and day already.

God, he was a goner.

He tried not to be too obvious about watching her

as she walked out the door and down the street to her next destination. Once she was out of sight, he faced Stella.

"I think I'd like to buy another print for my office."

Chapter Three

All during the rest of her errands, Elly smiled in anticipation of that night's outing. It was true—she did like Will's mother. But, honestly, she wanted to spend more time with this new and oh-so-improved Will Jackson.

Not until she was a couple of miles out of Cody on the way back to Markton did doubt creep past her happiness. Once planted, the thought that she'd made a mistake grew. She berated herself for agreeing to the dinner when everything was so unsettled at home. How could she go out and have an enjoyable evening when her family was going through such a rough patch? It felt wrong, heartless.

But as far as her parents knew, she wasn't supposed to know anything about her father's affair. Or what it might mean for her family. If she kept hanging around the ranch, even if she kept herself busy, she might accidentally let something slip. Maybe dinner with Will and his family was actually the best thing she could do right now. If she acted normal, maybe everything would work itself out.

She could hope, at least.

Her phone rang when she was halfway back to Markton. When she glanced at the caller ID, she almost didn't answer. Her nerves fired, making her grip the steering wheel tighter with her left hand. She hated this feeling of dread.

The phone rang a second time.

What if Mark and Janie had found out about the rumor, about Jesse looking into it? How would they react? What if Janie found out Elly knew what was going on and hadn't told her? Elly was not a fan of secrets and hated keeping this one. It gnawed at her, trying to carve an exit to the outside world.

When the phone rang a third time, Elly poised her thumb above the send button. She was supposed to be acting normal, right? She hit the button and answered.

"Hey. What's up?"

"Thrill a minute here at the land of feed and grain. What are you doing tonight?"

Okay, she didn't sound upset. In fact, she sounded a bit on the bored side. Chances were she was still in the dark about the supposed connection between J.W. and Mark. Elly sighed in thanks for her temporary reprieve.

"Actually, I'm going to a birthday dinner for Virginia Jackson."

"Really? How did that come about?"

"Will invited me."

"Will? When did you see him?"

Elly's heart jolted at the memory of her encountering Will the day before, why he'd been in her home. "Just now, in Cody. He lives there. Ran into him while I was dropping off stuff at the gallery."

"So, Billy the Kid is back," Janie said with amusement in her voice. "Where'd he go with his big brain after college?"

"I heard Denver. And I'm pretty sure we can't call him Billy the Kid anymore since he's a good half foot taller than me."

"Interesting that he's not back five minutes and he asks you out."

Her friend's assumption, as well as the teasing tone, surprised Elly.

"He didn't ask me out, you goober. It's a get-together for his mother."

"Uh-huh."

"What's that supposed to mean?"

"Just that it seems his crush hasn't gone anywhere since he left home."

Elly scrunched her forehead in confusion. "What are you talking about?"

Janie snorted. "Don't tell me you never realized Will had a crush on you. If it had been any more obvious, the boy would have been wearing a blinking billboard around his neck. I'm sure I must have teased you about it at some point."

"Have you been sniffing fertilizer or something?"

"No, I'm perfectly chemical-free. And very observant."

Elly thought back to when they'd all been younger, tried to remember if she'd ever noticed anything that could have been construed as a crush on Will's part. She hadn't even seen him much outside of school. His dad had worked at the ranch, but Will's allergies had been so bad that he couldn't spend much time there.

But he hadn't sneezed once yesterday, had he?

"Do you honestly not remember him asking you out?" Janie asked.

"What?"

"When Sean Barrett dumped you right before prom, Will offered to take you."

"He was kidding around, trying to make me feel better."

"Was he?"

"Of course. He never asked again."

"Maybe because you laughed when he offered the first time."

"I did not."

"You did."

Elly tried to remember the specifics of that day, but all she could recall clearly was how mad she'd been at Sean for being such a jerk.

"Even if Will did have a crush, that was years ago."

"This is Markton. It doesn't change, and neither do the people."

"He lives in Cody."

"Yeah, big difference. Well, call me later. I want to hear all the details of your date."

"It's not a date."

"Well, it's suddenly rush hour for feed. Toodles," Janie said, totally ignoring Elly's assertion.

Elly closed and tossed the phone onto the seat beside her, glad she'd made it through the conversation without giving any hint that anything was wrong. But she worried about having to face Janie. Her friend was smart, and probably knew Elly better than her brothers did. Janie would figure out something was wrong and question Elly until she caved and told her. And then everything would change.

Elly didn't think it was going to be for the better.

AFTER A GOOD WORKOUT with Pepper, in which she shaved a little more off her time, Elly indulged in a longer-than-usual shower complete with a new bottle of sweet-pea body wash. Wrapped in a towel, she sat on the edge of her bed and stared at the clothes hanging in her closet. She didn't have what one would call an extensive dating wardrobe. Jeans and Western button-up shirts, check. Outfits more appropriate for business meetings, sure. But cute, date-worthy clothes? Not so much.

When would she use them anyway? Most of her "dates" were with guys she knew from the rodeo circuit, and her brothers watched her and any dates with such intensity that it made a social life more trouble than it was worth most of the time.

But as she'd told Janie, this wasn't a date. She and Will hadn't spoken more than a handful of minutes in the past decade. He was two years younger than her, so they'd never even had a class together before they'd gone off to their respective colleges—he after his sophomore year, she more traditionally after her senior.

Not to mention the reason they'd even crossed paths now was because he'd been hired by Jesse. Wouldn't there be some sort of conflict-of-interest thing going there?

Scolding herself for thinking too much about what she wore to an outing that was most certainly not a date, she rose and strode to the closet. She sifted through the offerings beyond the collection of red shirts she wore in every rodeo and found a fluffy white sweater.

She pulled it out of the closet and held it up to herself as she faced the full-length mirror on the closet door. With some dressy jeans and her red heels, it'd be a good choice for a non-date evening when she wanted to show up looking nice, but not too nice like she was trying too hard to impress.

Geez. Why had Janie planted that crush idea in her head? Wasn't it enough that she'd already been thinking way too much about Will anyway? She felt like she was fifteen again, when she'd had an all-consuming crush on Brent Crayton, a steer wrestler from Kingsville, Texas.

She deliberately forced herself to think about other things—her next Cottonwood Chronicles blog post about the changing of seasons on the ranch, travel plans for the next rodeo, what photos she wanted to print and take to the gallery next since she'd evidently had two more sales today. Anything to keep her from thinking about how tall and handsome Will had grown—and how weird it was to think of him in the way she was.

It was no use though. Every time she forced her train

of thought down one track, it always chugged along for a short time before derailing back to Will. Maybe avoiding dating wasn't such a good idea if the mere idea of sitting at the same table with a good-looking guy affected her so much.

She stopped applying makeup and stared at herself in the bathroom mirror. Thinking about Will sure was better than dwelling on the situation with her dad and Mark though. What could it hurt to just enjoy the scenery? No one had to know but her. And she could think of worse things to serve as a distraction.

With a shake of her head, she left the bathroom and slipped silver hoops in her ears. The sound of male laughter from the main part of the house signaled that her brothers had already started playing poker. Normally, she'd be sitting in with them, and usually holding her own, if she wasn't with Janie or doing something with her new sisters-in-law. She sighed and wondered if she could just sneak out her window to avoid the inevitable barrage of questions.

She rolled her eyes at herself as she headed toward the collective sound of the brothers Cody.

"That's an odd outfit for poker," Dex said when he glanced up from his cards.

"That's because I'm not playing poker tonight. Got other plans," she said as casually as she could.

Dusty, Dex's twin, made a sour face at his cards and tossed them facedown on the table. "Where are you and Janie off to now?"

"I'm not going out with Janie." She didn't explain

further, deciding that she'd at least make them work for every little scrap of information. Where was the fun in making it easy?

When she noticed the suspicion on her brothers' faces, she wondered if maybe her tactic was ill advised.

"I'm going to a birthday party for Virginia Jackson."

Surprise tugged at Dusty's face. "Really?"

"Yes, really."

"Why?" Walker asked.

Elly propped her hands on her hips. "Because she's a nice lady. And because Will asked me." Dang, she shouldn't have said the last part. Already the guys were shifting in their seats, probably ready to forsake poker to escort her.

Then she made the bigger mistake of meeting the gaze of the only brother who hadn't spoken. Jesse eyed her with veiled disapproval, but not enough that it'd be obvious to anyone who didn't know why she and Will had crossed paths again. Thankfully, his desire to keep the situation with their father quiet prevented him from questioning her like he normally would.

"We playing or not?" he asked as he turned his attention back to the cards.

Before the others could recover from the shock of Jesse missing an opportunity to make her feel like she was fifteen and completely ignorant of the male gender, she grabbed her coat and headed out the door.

She didn't slow down until she turned off the ranch road onto the highway.

"THERE SHE IS." Virginia Jackson gave an enthusiastic wave across the restaurant.

Will was careful not to show how his heart rate kicked up at the knowledge that Elly had arrived. After impulsively buying two more of her photographs for his office that afternoon, he'd forced himself to go back to work and apply all his attention to the two cases he'd acquired besides Jesse Cody's. He'd actually done pretty well—if you considered thinking about Elly half a dozen times an hour versus a dozen pretty well.

His mom and Aunt Judith stood, his mom opening her arms to give Elly a big hug. "It's so good to see you. I haven't talked to you in forever."

Elly wrapped Virginia in a hug, like it was the highlight of her day, then did the same with Judith. If that didn't make him like her more, he didn't possess a law degree. A bit more of the resentment—the resentment he'd harbored so deep he hadn't realized it—slipped away.

When she turned to face him, for a moment he reveled in the idea that she might hug him, too.

"Hey, Will. Long time, no see."

He smiled while he told himself a hug between them would have just been awkward. "Eons," he said, to which she swatted him playfully on the upper arm.

Before she could take a seat, he pulled her chair out for her. He purposely didn't meet his mother's or aunt's eyes. He'd been back in Wyoming about two seconds before they'd started trying to match him up with someone. If he'd thought tonight's scenario through, he would have realized it hadn't been his smartest move.

Though as he seated himself across from Elly, he couldn't be sorry. All the questions and matchmaking attempts were an insignificant price to pay for getting to spend the evening in the company of a beautiful woman. As unwise as that might end up being.

They put conversation on hold when the waitress arrived to take their orders. But as soon as the young girl left, his mom patted Elly on her hands, where they rested on the table.

"Honey, I've been following all your successes. Sounds like this could be your year."

Elly's eyes brightened like a child's right before opening a tantalizingly huge gift on Christmas morning. "I hope so. We've certainly been training hard."

"You'll make it. I feel it," Virginia said. She turned to Will. "A month from now, our Elly will be a national champion barrel racer."

Our Elly. He liked the sound of that.

"We'll see," Elly said before he could reply. "It all comes down to how well we do in Denver."

His mom waved off Elly's modesty. "Girl, I've been watching you ride since you were no taller than this table. Sam used to say you and a horse seemed to become one when you rode."

Will tried to ignore a twinge of hurt, something he'd never shared with anyone. He could imagine his father saying something like that about Elly with awe in his voice. Sam Jackson had loved all things rodeo, had yearned to make the big time himself. But his bronc-riding talent had taken him only as far as small, non-PRCA rodeos.

And though he'd never voiced it, Will suspected his father had been disappointed that Will hadn't chosen that as his dream himself. Will couldn't have followed it anyway because of his severe allergies. Sometimes he'd gotten the feeling his father saw him as weak, as a poor reflection of himself. Sure, they'd had a decent relationship, but it hadn't been really close. They couldn't have been any more different.

"Okay, enough about me," Elly said, breaking into Will's memories and meeting his gaze. "I'm not the only talented person at the table. I heard you were top of your college class when you graduated." She smiled and lifted an eyebrow. "Not bad for someone two years younger than everyone else."

He soaked in how she smiled when she said it, like he wasn't some sort of oddity walking around with an oversize brain. When she looked at him now, he felt like she really saw him. So different from when they'd gone to school together. He noticed his mom and aunt shift into matching "we're going to tell a tale" positions.

"You've done it now," he said under his breath.

Elly's expression shifted to one of confusion. "What?"

She found out over the next few minutes as the two women enumerated his many academic accomplishments, both as an undergrad and while in law school at the University of Colorado. A couple of times, Elly met his eyes and smiled in amusement. He gave her what he hoped was a look that promised well-planned retribution.

"He was asked to join a big law firm in Denver, but he came back home." Virginia beamed with pride.

"It's the Park County nightlife," Elly said. "It's hard to resist."

Will laughed. "Nightlife isn't even on the radar. I'm more concerned about keeping clients coming through the front door."

"Oh, don't worry," Virginia said. "Once word gets around about your practice, they'll be lining up down the street."

His mom, bless her, had a very inflated idea of his attractiveness as legal counsel. His age and the newness of his law degree could cause people to second-guess his ability. He'd just be happy to pay the bills and have enough left over to eat. The last thing he should have been doing was buying expensive artwork, but he'd eat ramen noodles and macaroni and cheese for a year before he'd part with Elly's photographs.

His mom looked on the verge of more bragging when he spotted their waitress approaching the table with a large tray. He'd never been so happy to see a plate of food arrive.

"Saved by steak and potatoes!"

Elly laughed as his mom and Judith scolded him.

"We're proud of you," Judith said.

"I'm your mother, I'm old, and you just have to put up with it."

"I know."

Elly, perhaps taking pity on him, steered the conversation away from him by asking, "So, what have you two been up to lately?"

As they all ate, his mom and aunt filled Elly in on their activities with the local quilters' guild and their weekly trip to see a movie.

"We're considering taking a little trip somewhere," his mom said. "Hey, maybe we should go to Denver and watch you ride. That'd be exciting."

"We could see her when she makes the National Finals Rodeo," Judith said.

His mother looked at him. "And Will could go, too. Oh, this is going to be so much fun."

"So your allergies don't bother you anymore?" Elly asked.

Great, she remembered one of his weaknesses, the thing that had kept him from going to the Cottonwood with his dad more often.

"Oh, he doesn't have to worry about those anymore," his mom said.

"Better living through pharmacology," he said.

"He's quite the outdoorsman now. Always going climbing or kayaking or some such. Even rides a horse now and then."

"We should go riding sometime," Elly said.

Will felt like he'd slipped into an alternate reality. But in any reality, he loved the idea of riding alongside Elly, showing how he wasn't the weak, dorky kid she'd once known. But he decided on a noncommittal answer.

"Maybe." He didn't want to seem too eager and revert back to that geeky Billy the Kid. That's not how he wanted her to see him at all.

His skin warmed when he let himself think about exactly how he *did* want her to see him.

ELLY HAD A GREAT TIME at dinner, much more so than she'd even anticipated. Virginia and Judith were adorable in how they tag-teamed to be the Will Jackson fan club. And he was cute because of how embarrassed it made him even though he tried to hide it.

Wicked smart, a devoted outdoor sports enthusiast, quite frankly gorgeous, and she suspected the kind of man who moved back to Wyoming to help out his widowed mother and aunt despite his claim he wanted to try a small-town practice. Why on earth did his mother and aunt feel they had to market him? Why hadn't some smart woman snapped him up already?

The idea of him with another woman didn't sit well with her, as irrational as that seemed.

She didn't realize she was staring at him until he looked up from paying the check and met her eyes. Though she should have broken eye contact, she didn't. This new Will Jackson fascinated her, had gotten under her skin more quickly than any man ever had.

"This is just gorgeous," Virginia said as she admired her framed moose photo again. "Elly, honey, you are a woman of many talents."

She shifted her eyes away from Will to his mother. "I'm glad you like it."

With dinner finished and long hours ahead the next day, Elly acknowledged the fact that she needed to go home. Though she'd much rather stay here and find out more about Will the man than go home and no doubt have to face Jesse. She sighed inwardly.

"Much as I hate to leave good company, I need to be getting home." She shifted and grabbed her purse.

"It's about time for all of us to vacate the premises," Virginia said as she scooted her chair back.

The four of them headed for the door, but Virginia and Judith detoured toward the restroom.

"You two go on," Virginia said. "We'll be out in a bit."

Elly wasn't fooled in the least. She knew attempted matchmaking when she saw it. She chuckled a little as she headed out the door ahead of Will. She didn't say anything as they walked toward the line of cars at the edge of the parking lot. When they reached hers, she turned and found Will closer than she expected. Her breath caught for a moment before she convinced her lungs to function properly again.

"Thanks for dinner. And thanks for inviting me."

"You're welcome. Sorry they went on and on."

Elly laughed. "They're sweet. It's nice to have people who love you enough that they're willing to sing your praises in embarrassing detail."

He gave her a crooked smile, and in the half light of the parking lot she thought she'd never seen a sexier face on a man. He'd be shocked if he knew how much effort it was taking her to keep from stepping forward and kissing him.

That thought shook her. She broke eye contact and opened the door of her car. "Well, thanks again."

He nodded, and she got into the car before she could act on her uncharacteristic impulses. The fact that he watched her drive away didn't help, making her wonder if he'd been thinking similar thoughts. Had Janie been right about that crush? Could such a thing, if it ever existed, have survived all those years?

She shook her head as she pulled out onto the street. Will Jackson wasn't a good idea right now, not when he was in the middle of determining whether she had another brother and what that would mean to her family.

But the urge to turn around and give in to her impulses dogged her all the way back to the ranch.

Chapter Four

Will dreamed about Elly all night after their dinner, then several times again the next night. Sweet dreams where she simply turned and looked at him with a beautiful smile. Dreams where they were riding horseback through the mountains, side by side. And then there were the dreams that left his heart pumping and other parts of him demanding satisfaction.

He shook his head as he drove toward the Cottonwood Ranch, scolding himself for not being stronger in the face of her temptation. He'd changed so much in his life. Why couldn't he cure his attraction to her like he had his allergic reactions? If only there was an anti-infatuation pill.

How was he going to face her and not think about the dreams he'd had the night before? Would his inner dork come out and cause him to turn ten shades of red?

The entrance to the ranch came into view. He slowed then waited for a dualie pickup hitched to a new trailer to pull out of the ranch road. He waved at the driver and glanced at the truck's door as it passed. Longstreet

Ranch—Billings, Montana. Looked like the Codys had sold a couple more quarter horses.

Once the ranch road was clear, he made the turn through the large metal gate under the giant arch of elk and deer horns and tried for the millionth time to figure out what he was going to say to Elly when he saw her. If he saw her. There was no guarantee she was even at the ranch, though he certainly hoped so.

When he arrived at the old homestead, he parked and ran up the front steps. He knocked but no one answered. He'd raised his hand to knock again when he heard the sound of hooves running. Will walked to the end of the porch and looked out across the ranch. No running horses in sight. But then he noticed the big door open at the end of the practice barn.

He listened closer and realized he recognized the rhythm of hoofbeats as those of a horse rounding barrels. Instead of turning toward the ranch's main office to see if Jesse was there, he gave in to temptation and headed toward the barn. He used to love to watch her ride, and he doubted that had changed, either. But now he wouldn't make a fool of himself by breaking out in a fit of sneezing.

When he entered the barn, he spotted her immediately.

She stroked the big black horse's shiny neck as she steered the animal out of the end of the arena. Will watched as she lined the horse up for another go at the barrels. As she kicked the animal into a full-on run, Will held his breath as she flew across the starting line and headed for the first barrel. Despite the fact she'd spent her entire life on a horse, he couldn't help the moment of fear when he saw her speed, the difference in size between her and the animal she rode. His heart beat hard as she urged the horse tightly around the barrel, her inside boot nearly dragging the ground.

She rounded the first barrel, giving it a good shave as she remained in total control of her powerful beast. Barrel two danced a little as she circled it, but it stayed upright. As she flew by, she was nothing but a blur of blue denim and green shirt, her braid flying out behind her. She and the mare seemed like one animal as she rounded the last barrel and raced back to the starting gate.

A glance at the time caused her to whoop. Elly leaned forward and hugged the horse's neck then guided her into a cooldown walk around the outer edge of the arena.

Elly had been so much in her own world that she hadn't noticed him until they were halfway up the side where he stood. When she smiled, his heart leaped for an entirely different reason.

"You sure that horse doesn't have wings?" he asked as he approached the fence circling the practice arena.

She laughed, a musical sound with a hint of mischief. "Now that might come in handy."

The horse sniffed at him, so Will reached over the fence and let the animal smell his hand. "Don't think you need wings. You were already flying."

"I'm going to have to if I want to win in Denver."

He looked up at her flushed face, at the wisps of hair that had escaped her braid. "Do you have to win there to get to the Finals?"

She shrugged. "Depends on how everyone else does, but I want the win to be on the safe side. Not to mention, I have different bets with every one of my brothers that makes winning imperative. If I don't win, they'll be impossible to be around."

"What kind of bets?"

"Let's see. Money, a month of cooking, something totally embarrassing I'm not about to share."

He laughed as he reached up and gave her horse an affectionate scratch on her forehead. "What's her name?"

"Pepper. I've had this pretty girl about four years now, since I had to retire Cranberry."

He remembered the roan mare. He'd probably seen Elly astride that horse as much as he'd seen her off it.

"She's a powerful animal."

"Yeah," she said as she ran her fingers through Pepper's coal mane. "Feels like riding a stick of dynamite sometimes, but it's like we've got one brain. She responds so well to my commands, sometimes I swear before I do more than think them."

"Are you nervous?" he asked.

Her forehead scrunched. "About what?"

"Being this close to the Finals? You've worked toward this for so long."

A moment of surprise passed across her face before she broke eye contact. "No, not really. Not guaranteeing what I'll feel like when I get to Denver, but not now. I just focus on practicing really hard."

"Your brothers in the hunt this year?"

"Jesse's made the NFR. He and…" Her words faded away, causing Will to look up at her again.

"What?"

She wrapped her hands more tightly around Pepper's reins. "He and Mark Hansen are both in the running for the bull-riding title."

He nodded at the awkwardness of that situation. Sad that the fact two riders from tiny Markton reaching that level of success in rodeo's premiere event couldn't be celebrated—at least not by the Cody siblings.

Will hated the pall that descended over their conversation and wished he could rewind time, erase words.

"Are you here to see Jesse?" Was it possible he detected a bit of nervousness on her part? He didn't dare allow himself to think it might have anything to do with him.

He nodded. "I didn't have an appointment, but I was on my way back from Cheyenne and thought I'd check in."

She looked on the verge of asking a question before she closed her mouth and glanced toward the open door. "He had a lunch meeting. I don't know when he's supposed to be back." She returned her gaze to him. "Would you like to come in for some coffee while you wait?"

"That sounds good." In lieu of holding her and making all her sorrows go away, he'd take coffee and conversation. It was so much more than he'd ever had with her before. He knew he should have passed on her offer, but damned if he had the ability to do so.

She nodded toward the house. "The door's unlocked. Go on in. I'll be in as soon as I take care of Pepper."

Elly guided Pepper away from the fence and slowly toward the entrance to the arena. Will watched her, admiring how natural she looked in the saddle. Of course she did. She was a Cody, part of the first family of Wyoming ranching and rodeoing. She'd been on a horse probably before she could talk.

When she rode out of sight, he made his way toward the house. But once inside, he felt like an intruder. For several seconds, he just stood in the foyer, gazing at the photographs and paintings on the walls. For some reason, he remembered one of the few times his dad had brought him to the ranch. The entire Cody family had lived in this house then. It'd been winter, and a big fire had been roaring in the stone fireplace.

His dad had deposited him in front of the fireplace while he disappeared into the office to talk to J. W. Cody. The same office where Will had met with Jesse a few days ago. He'd stood there in front of the fire, his back half-toasty, and watched the Cody clan bent over a Scrabble board on the kitchen table. He'd wondered what it was like to be part of such a big family, to have siblings.

As they'd finished a game, Anne Cody, Elly's mom, had noticed him and invited him to join them. He still remembered the sting as Dex and Dusty had complained that he would just beat them and how Elly had swatted

Dusty on the shoulder hard enough to make him complain about that, too. Part of Will had been thankful while another had been embarrassed a girl had taken up for him like he was helpless.

"Okay, new game. Let's play teams. Will's with me," Elly had said and smiled a knowing smile at him.

That was all it took for him to fall irrevocably in love with her. Sitting beside her, spelling out one high-scoring word after another, had been like ten Christmases rolled into one.

Will stepped away from the memory and back into the present by heading toward the kitchen. Not much had changed, and the coffeemaker, though a newer model, sat in the same spot. He took off his jacket and started making coffee.

That task finished, he wandered around the main room. Picking out the photos Elly had taken was easy now. Strange how viewing only a few of her shots at the gallery had given him a sense of how she looked at the world. She found beauty in simplicity, in nature, in family. Animals, people, flowers, waterways all came alive through her lens.

He made his way around the room and back to the kitchen. He glanced out the window toward the barns, watched as the hands went about their work with the horses and unloading feed, as another horse trailer backed up to the corrals. If he hadn't been allergic to animals, would he have ended up working here like his father? Would he have caved to that path and not gone to college? Or would the sting of Elly's rejection when he'd finally gotten up the nerve to ask her out still have sent him fleeing from Markton and the Cottonwood Ranch as fast as he could?

Ranch life had its appeal, but he was happy with the life he'd chosen. He liked helping people. And he liked the stronger person he'd become by leaving—even if that strength was shaken every time he was near Elly. He really should go. Before he made a step to do so, Elly came in the back door, the gust of air that accompanied her causing the rich aroma of freshly brewed coffee to fill the room.

"You didn't actually have to *make* the coffee," she said as she removed her jacket and hung it on a hook by the door.

"I don't mind."

When she moved closer and reached up into the cabinet for two mugs, he inhaled her scent—a mixture of horse, earth and something flowery. So very Elly. He quelled the urge to smooth the loose hair at her temples.

Desire pumped through him with such power that he had to step away from her or risk really embarrassing himself.

She handed him a steaming mug and headed for the table. When she slid into the nearest chair, he took the one adjacent to her. He kept his hands wrapped around the mug to keep them from wandering where they wanted to go.

"So, tell me about what's been going on with you since you left Markton," she said.

He chuckled. "I think you heard it all at dinner the other night."

"I got the proud mama and auntie version. I want to hear yours. Like how was college as a sixteen-year-old?"

He shrugged. "Okay." Lonely, but he wasn't going to say that and look like a big loser.

"How did you decide on law?"

"Will you think less of me if I say it was because I had a crush on a girl in pre-law?"

She placed her hand above her heart. "You have wrecked all my illusions of your noble aspirations."

"Nice drama," he said. "Too bad Markton doesn't have a theater."

She laughed and took a sip of her coffee. "So, did you follow the girl to law school?"

"No. She dropped out of the program, but by then I'd taken enough courses that I found I actually liked it."

"You know, it fits."

"How so?"

"You were always so smart, good with puzzles and logic, figuring stuff out. I can see how the law might be just a big, complicated puzzle."

"I've never heard anyone put it that way, but yeah."

She leaned back in her chair. "Plus, I'm sure it had to help with the ladies. Lots of women like their doctors and lawyers."

"But not you?" God, had he just said that out loud? She tilted her head. "What makes you say that?"

Think fast, genius. "You said, 'Lots of women' like you weren't among them."

She lowered her gaze to her mug and fiddled with the handle. "I don't have anything against them. Well, most of them. Those ambulance chasers get on my last nerve. Bottom feeders, every last one of them."

"Yeah. You know, I could tell which of my classmates were going to go that route from the first day. They went into law for the money. Not for the challenge or to help people."

When he looked up, she was watching him and smiling.

"What?"

"You'd do it for free, wouldn't you?"

Her question surprised him and filled him with pride that she would think so highly of him. It managed to erase a little more of the past hurt he'd suffered at her hand. "If I could afford to, probably. But hey, a guy's gotta eat."

"Speaking of which…" Elly stood and went to the counter, retrieved a round tin and returned to the table. "You've got to try these. Mom made them this morning. They're my favorite." She opened the lid and picked out a chocolate chip cookie, extended it toward him.

When he reached for it, his fingers brushed hers. Their eyes met for a suspended moment before she looked away and then picked out a cookie for herself. He took a bite to redirect his mind and was surprised when he tasted orange, as well.

"Good," he said around a mouthful of cookie.

"Too good. I have to keep busy so I don't sit here and scarf down the entire tin."

"There are worse things to indulge in."

"But few as fattening. I'd be as big as one of the barns."

"I doubt that." He suspected his words were too telling when she caught his gaze and looked like she was trying to read his mind. "So, what about you? Besides rodeo, what keeps Elly Cody busy these days?"

Another moment passed before she broke eye contact and reached for a second cookie. "I'm the IT and PR departments all rolled into one. I maintain the Web site, a blog, community outreach, conduct tours. Oh…" She looked at her watch. "In fact, I'm supposed to give a tour in about thirty minutes."

When she looked up again, she had a smear of chocolate at the corner of her mouth. Before he could tell himself not to, Will reached over and wiped the chocolate away with his finger. Elly's mouth parted, but before she could say anything the front door opened and a gust of chilly air brought Will back to his senses.

He looked over his shoulder to see Jesse Cody standing in the foyer, door still open at his back, his eyes glued on the scene in front of him. Will thought this would be the part of the movie where the guy in his position gulped. But instead, he met Jesse's gaze and leaned back in his chair.

Elly spoke first. "Close the door, dude. Mom swears up and down you weren't born in the barn, but I'm not convinced."

Will glanced back at her and smiled. He heard the door close behind him, but he couldn't look away from her. At least not until she gave him a small smile back, making him feel like he could face any Cody brother, no matter how big and imposing.

WHEN WILL RETURNED HIS attention to Jesse, Elly nearly rolled her eyes at the look on her brother's face. She'd seen it any time a guy had expressed interest in her. Jesse and her other brothers had a way of saying things to guys that made them decide she wasn't worth having to deal with the Cody men.

Would Will be as intimidated?

For a moment, she pictured Will running that gauntlet with a smile on his handsome face and a look of determination to get to her. The image was so powerful, her hand fumbled her mug and she nearly spilled her coffee.

She made the mistake of meeting Jesse's gaze. Her blunder hadn't gone unnoticed.

"Well, I've got to get ready for a tour." Even though she wanted to look at Will again, she resisted. Instead, she played as if no unexpected emotions were swirling inside her and retreated to her room.

Once inside, she closed the door and dropped to the side of her bed.

What was going on with her? The moment Will had touched the edge of her mouth, a zing had ricocheted through her body. She had to get a grip and realize he was probably just being nice.

Maybe she was reading too much into his invitation to dinner, into looks and kind gestures, into Janie's assertion that Will had liked her once upon a time. But if that was true and she'd rejected him, what were the odds he'd give her a second chance? He'd said nothing romantic, had not asked her out on a date, hadn't attempted to kiss her when they'd stood near each other as she'd poured coffee as many guys might have.

Besides, he was two years younger than her.

Now, why did that matter?

It doesn't.

She flopped back on the bed and stared at the ceiling, strained to hear his voice. But all she heard was a faint rumble, Will's and Jesse's voices indistinguishable from each other through two doors. She wondered if Jesse had dived right into the business at hand or if he'd said something about her.

Why was she torturing herself when she didn't even know if Will thought of her as more than a girl he'd once known, maybe had had a teenage crush on? She could be no more to him than the sister of a client.

That thought stopped her. She'd known why he'd come to the ranch, and yet she hadn't asked him if he'd learned anything. Granted, he might not have told her since he'd technically been hired by Jesse, but she hadn't even asked.

Other questions, ones totally unrelated to Mark's parentage, had somehow overridden what she should be concerned about. How could she think about how Will made her heart rate pick up when he could be the harbinger of news that might split her family apart? News that could cost Elly her best friend.

She had to start thinking of Will as her brother's legal counsel, not as the first guy in a long time to make her yearn for what was missing from her life. She needed to focus on her family, on the Finals. Not on how she wanted to find out what Will Jackson's lips felt like on hers.

The sound of a bus pulling up outside made her close her eyes and wish she could disappear. Normally, she liked conducting tours of the ranch, talking about her family's rich heritage in this part of Wyoming and the realities of modern ranching.

But this was the first time she had to wonder if there was more to the Cody heritage than she'd believed all her life. That maybe she had another brother, one who because of his age could claim the position of the firstborn.

Chapter Five

Elly made it through the tour, relying on experience to recite details and answer questions. Normally she enjoyed learning where everyone was from, what they did for a living and what had brought them to Wyoming. Usually it was Yellowstone or the Big Horn Mountains, but occasionally someone would surprise her with a different response.

No surprises today, and honestly not much interest on her part. She'd spent as much time thinking about her family's situation and her attraction to Will as she had the stops on the tour. When she waved goodbye to the bus full of tourists, exhaustion pressed down on her.

She glanced toward the house and noticed Will's vehicle still sitting outside. Despite the fact she wanted to see him again, the topic of conversation in that house caused her to turn and walk in the other direction. She hopped into one of the golf carts they used to zip around the ranch and was halfway to her parents' house before she realized where she was going. She waved to Barbara, her parents' longtime housekeeper, as the older woman passed by in her car.

The main house was a gorgeous work of architecture that had graced the covers of half a dozen magazines. Walker's wife, Paula, had supplied the spectacular landscaping. Even though Elly could appreciate all the grandeur, she preferred the homestead house where she'd grown up right down in the thick of things.

What type of house did Will live in? Or was it an apartment?

Elly shook her head as she parked and headed in through the double front doors. As she skirted the huge cowboy statue in the foyer, she combated the desire to talk to her mom about Will and her unexpected feelings toward him. But Will wasn't a good topic to broach with her mom, not when Elly knew the reason Will was even at Cottonwood was because Anne Cody's husband had been unfaithful.

She stopped halfway through the house and took a deep breath, tried to think of things to talk about with her mom that would be light, happy, with no hint of Mark Hansen or Will Jackson. The scents of baking announced not only where her mom was but also the fact that she was still upset.

As Elly approached the doorway into the kitchen, she doubted anything she said was going to lift her mother's mood. Anne sat at the table, surrounded by baking pans of all sizes and shapes; bags of flour, sugar and chocolate chips; a large can of cooking spray; and two opened cookbooks. One of the cookbooks sat right in front of her, but Elly doubted her mother was paying attention to the ingredients list or instructions because she was too busy sniffling and using a tissue to dab at her eyes.

Elly's heart broke for her mom. She'd never been as furious with her father as she was the moment she saw her mom's tears. Anne seemed unusually fragile, as though she might crumble like a too-dry cookie.

When Elly stepped into the room, Anne jumped then hurried to dry her eyes and put on a brave face.

Elly slipped into the chair opposite her mother and wrapped her hand around one of her mom's. "I'm sorry."

Anne looked up and met her only daughter's eyes then her shoulders slumped. "You know."

Elly nodded, but she didn't offer an explanation of how she knew or ask any questions. This wasn't something she was going to push her mom to talk about, especially not when her mom looked so sad and hurt.

Anne slipped her hand out from between Elly's and rose to her feet. She moved the cookbook to the countertop beside the stove. Next she pulled together the makings of what looked like it would become a lemon bundt cake. If there were a less heartwrenching reason behind the baking, Elly would have looked forward to the result.

"What do you know?" her mom asked, pretending to study the recipe.

Elly swallowed and forced herself to stay seated when everything was telling her to go to her mother and wrap her arms around her, to offer comfort. But she suspected her mom really would fall apart then, that contact with anyone would shatter the precarious hold she had on herself.

"That...that Dad had an affair, that he might be Mark Hansen's father."

Anne nodded.

"Is it true?" Elly's question came out as a choked whisper.

Anne stopped mixing ingredients and stared down into the bowl. For several seconds, she said nothing. "We believe so. Your father has told Mark as much," she whispered finally.

"The bastard," Elly said under her breath.

"It was a long time ago. We went through a difficult period after I miscarried."

Elly knew there had been a baby before Jesse, one her mom had lost at three months. Her mother rarely mentioned the baby or how she'd fallen apart after the loss. Each year, on the day of the miscarriage, Anne always seemed sadder.

Anger welled up inside Elly. How could her father have betrayed her mother when she'd been hurting so much? All her respect and admiration for her father disintegrated around her. She wanted to scream and curse, but now wasn't the time or place.

"Don't say anything to your father," Anne said.

"Why not?" Elly couldn't prevent the bitterness that coated her question. She felt as if it was oozing out of her pores.

Anne looked back over her shoulder. "This is something your father and I have to handle."

The knowledge of what was going on at the homestead right at that moment weighed on Elly. She didn't like keeping anything from her mom. Being the only girl, she and her mom had always been close. Close enough that she could well imagine what it must have been like to find out her husband had not only had an affair but had fathered a child with another woman, a child who was the brother of her daughter's best friend. No wonder she was sitting at the kitchen table alone, crying. Living next to a lie did that to a person.

God, she didn't want to talk about this anymore. Didn't even want to think about it.

"Do you need any help?"

Anne shook her head. "Honestly, if you don't mind, I think I'd like to be alone."

The words would have hurt if Elly didn't know this was how her mom always dealt with major upsets. She baked and wanted to be alone with her own thoughts until she sorted through things.

"Okay," Elly said, but it took her several moments to force herself to her feet and walk out of the kitchen. She paused at the doorway and looked back at her mother. "I love you, Mom."

Anne met her gaze and gave her a sad smile. "I love you too, honey. Now, go ride or something. Days are ticking away until Denver."

Even amidst all the turmoil in her own life, Anne was able to think about her children and what was important to them. It's what made her such a wonderful mother.

Someone who should have never been betrayed.

Elly trudged toward the front door then outside. She stood on the edge of the front porch and let her gaze run over the miles of Cody land in all directions. This ranch was as much a part of her as the blood pumping through her body. If her father's mistake had endangered that, she'd never forgive him.

She tried to shake away the doubts, wanted desperately for this entire situation to not be true. Not because she disliked Mark. No, that was Jesse's department. But she ached for her father to have never done what he had.

Maybe everyone was wrong. Even if her dad had an affair, that didn't mean Mark was his son. After all, Tomas Hansen had raised Mark as his own. Wouldn't he have known otherwise? Maybe Jesse was right in his demand for proof.

Or maybe the knowledge that Mark wasn't his son was what had driven Tomas to drink.

Unbidden, memories of Abigail Hansen looking at her in an odd way rose to the surface. At first Elly had thought she'd imagined it. Later she'd attributed it to the onset of Abigail's Alzheimer's disease. Never had she suspected what might have truly been running through Abigail's head—that her son was a Cody, too, that he deserved the wealth and privilege as much as Elly and her brothers. Not the hard life he'd had with Tomas Hansen as a father.

She stepped off the porch and returned to the golf cart. The sound of her mother's pain echoed in her head as she drove back down the road toward the main area of the ranch. As she approached the homested, she noticed Will coming out of the house and heading for his Yukon. Quick and irrational anger exploded within her at his involvement. She just wanted all of this to go away, to have never seen the light of day. But here Will was digging for a truth and consequences she didn't think she wanted to know.

How could she look at Will and not think about what had brought him back into her life? He'd be tainted, and she wanted him to remain untouched by the ugliness of the situation. Maybe she could convince Jesse to hire another attorney so she could look at Will without thinking about her father in Abigail Hansen's arms.

Of course, that was assuming that she'd have the opportunity and a reason to look at Will if he wasn't working for her brother.

Despite everything, she found she wanted that very much.

ELLY SAW DAWN MAKE ITS stealthy way onto the Cottonwood for the beginning of another day. She sat on the porch, a thick quilt wrapped around her and a steaming mug of coffee in her hand. A night of tossing and turning made her feel like something found on the bottom of a boot, but she'd given up sleeping an hour before daybreak.

She'd dragged herself out of bed and did her Web site and blog work for the day, checked the tour schedule and sent some e-mails regarding the upcoming Last Chance Trail Ride. The Cottonwood Ranch hosted the event for the locals each year before the heavy snows blanketed the mountains and valleys around Markton.

Movement at the edge of the fog still clinging to the ground caught her attention. When Jesse came into view astride Sundae, it surprised her. She'd thought he was still in bed and had envied him for it.

She could tell when he noticed her because he hesitated, pulling back on Sundae's reins, probably without thinking. But he started moving again after only the span of a breath.

"You couldn't sleep, either, huh?" she said when he came close enough to hear her.

"I've had better nights." He dismounted in a sliding motion that made her think it had been a great many nights since her brother had slept well.

"Was it something Will said?"

"Please, not this early."

"I have a right to know, Jess."

He sighed and rested one hand against Sundae's saddle horn as if he needed the horse's presence to keep him upright. "Nothing new."

Elly thought of what her mother had said about J.W., believing he was Mark's father. She wondered if Jesse had any inkling, but she couldn't bring herself to tell him.

"You two sure talked a long time for there to be nothing new."

"Give it a rest, okay. I just want five damn minutes where I don't have to think about this." He palmed Sundae's reins and headed toward the barn.

Didn't she want the same thing? To not think about the fact that Mark Hansen might be her half brother. Was that even possible?

Her quiet morning shattered, she headed into the house for a shower and a breakfast she suspected she wouldn't even taste.

Later, when she ran into Paco in the barn and learned he was headed into town for a load of feed, she offered to go instead. She had to get away from the ranch for a while.

When she arrived at the Feed and Grain with her order in hand, however, she wished she'd stayed at home. One look at Janie's drawn face and she feared the cause. A painful lump formed in Elly's throat, and for the first time in her life she didn't want to walk the final steps toward her best friend.

But she did. And the closer she got, the more she could see that Janie looked as if she was trying hard to hide her sadness. Just going through the motions to get through the day.

"Elly," Janie said when she spotted her. So much distance in that word.

"Hey."

"You need something?"

Elly bit her lip to keep it from trembling as she handed over the list of supplies she'd come to pick up.

Janie looked it over and nodded. "We should have all of this in stock." She started to walk away.

"Janie?"

The girl who'd been her closest confidante for as

long as she could remember stopped but didn't make eye contact.

"I don't know what to say," Elly said, wishing the right words to make everything okay would magically land on her tongue.

Janie met her eyes then. "You know?"

"I found out a few days ago."

"But you knew the last time I talked to you."

Elly nodded.

Janie let her breath out in a long exhale. "So no more secrets."

"Secrets?" There was something odd about what Janie had said. "When did Mark tell you?"

Janie refused to make eye contact. "He didn't."

Elly glanced around to see if any of the other customers were near enough to hear their conversation. "My father?"

Janie swallowed visibly, like she was trying to work a grapefruit down her throat. "I've known for a while, before Mark."

Elly's breath caught in her chest. "How long?"

"Since Dad was sick."

Before Elly could question her further, Janie choked out, "I can't talk about this now," then turned and gave Elly's list to Leslie Pearsoll, who was just stepping out of his office.

"Take care of Elly. I've got to help Collum McKinney find a new pair of boots."

If Elly stood where she was any longer, she was going to cry and make a fool out of herself.

"Elly?" Leslie said, sounding worried.

"I'll be back in a few minutes to get my load." She spun on her boot heel and hurried out of the store. Once outside, she realized there was nowhere to hide to get her emotions under control, to wrap her mind around the fact that Janie had known about the affair, about Mark, for months. How had she acted like nothing was wrong? And why the change in her behavior now? Was the news going to be made public? Elly's stomach rolled at the thought.

She spotted the Sagebrush Diner across the street and stalked toward it, pushed her way through the front door and up to the counter.

"Hey, Elly," Martha Pickens said from her post behind the cash register.

Elly just nodded and ordered a monster, one of the diner's signature six-inch diameter sweet rolls, and a large black coffee. She paid, offered a perfunctory thanks and retraced her steps outside.

She nearly plowed into Will as she barreled through the door into a world that was blanketed with too much sunshine for her mood.

Will gripped her upper arms to steady her. "Hey. I thought I saw you go in a minute ago." He must have seen her expression because his changed to one of concern. "You okay?"

"No, I'm not, as a matter of fact," she snapped.

Will glanced around then steered her away from the restaurant entrance to the side of the building that wasn't lined with windows through which everyone in town could see her implode.

"I don't think you want to do this here."

"I don't want to do this at all. I want it to go the hell away."

Will held her hands lightly in his. "What happened?"

His voice sounded so gentle, so understanding that she had to swallow the lump that was increasing in size by the second.

She told him about the encounter at the Feed and Grain, about what she feared it meant.

"You don't know what it means yet," he said.

"Nothing good." She sighed. "I feel like I'm losing everything."

"You're not losing Janie. Things may be strained between you two for a while, but you'll work it out."

She looked him fully in the face for the first time since she'd nearly bowled him over. Was she seeing more than concern in those gorgeous eyes of his?

No. She couldn't handle this, not now. She pulled her hands away and crossed her arms, causing her paper bag full of sweet roll to crumple. She turned away from him. "I need to go. I've got a load of feed to take home."

She thought he might try to stop her, but he didn't. Despite her being the one who walked away, her heart broke a little more. She blinked several times. God, nothing made sense anymore.

She made it to the truck, called out for the feed to be

put on the Cottonwood's account. The truck's back tires spit gravel as she sped from the parking lot.

She'd driven the road between Markton and the ranch so many times that it allowed her to travel on autopilot. She didn't even think about where she was until she noticed the pull off that overlooked the ranch. After skidding to a halt on the side of the road, she let her gaze wander over all the undulations and colors of the land. Cody land.

Maybe Mark Hansen's land.

Her father's betrayal, Janie's secrets and her own yo-yoing feelings about Will all collided inside her and caused a sob to break free only to be followed by several more. The stunning view before her grew blurry as she finally allowed herself to cry. She slammed the heels of her hands against the steering wheel, letting the anger and hurt come out any way it could find an exit.

After a few minutes of indulging her self-pity, she dried her tears on the sleeve of her jacket and stared out across the valley below. She would not lose this land or her family, no matter what happened. She was a Cody. She'd fight for it if she had to.

Something didn't feel quite right about her train of thought, and she sat in the silence of the surrounding mountains trying to figure out why.

Because Mark had never struck her as the type to make a money grab, no matter how much he struggled. Of course, she'd never wanted for anything because of a lack of money, so how could she know how someone in that situation would truly think? When he'd found out about his true parentage, had he looked at the Cody wealth and felt only resentment? Like he'd been robbed of what was rightfully his? In a way, did he feel like her—like part of her life had been a lie?

She wondered why he and Janie hadn't said anything after they found out? How had the truth finally been acknowledged by both Mark and Elly's father? And what had Janie meant by knowing before Mark?

Elly closed her eyes and massaged her temples. The combination of crying, too little sleep and too many questions bombarding her brain was giving her an unbearable headache.

Deciding to push it all as far away as possible and focus on work, she put the truck in gear and headed for home. Thinking about the situation wasn't going to change anything.

The deed was already done.

Chapter Six

Will finished going over the financial documents for Cottonwood Enterprises so he'd have a firm grasp on what was at stake if Mark Hansen was indeed J. W. Cody's biological son. He'd known the Codys were wealthy, but he hadn't realized to what extent. No wonder Elly and her brothers had their own plane and often flew to rodeos instead of spending days on the road. They didn't have to.

But sometimes they did. And they didn't mind getting their hands dirty either, as evidenced the day before when he'd bumped into Elly while she was in town picking up a load of feed. She could have had Slim, Big Ben, Paco or any number of employees perform that task, but she'd done it herself.

He sat back in his chair and stared at the phone on his desk. How many times had he almost picked it up to call her? She was upset, and he wanted to shield her from everything that was causing her pain. But he couldn't do that, could he? Not when he was involved in the situation that was causing her pain, that would keep reminding her of what her father had done.

It wasn't a good idea to get any more involved with Elly Cody.

Delia walked into his office and deposited a roast beef sandwich on his desk. "You look like you could use a nap."

"Not a bad idea," he said.

She plopped down in the chair across from him and pulled a large order of onion rings from the paper bag she held. The hot, greasy smell made his mouth water.

"So, you going on the trail ride this weekend?" she asked then took a bite of her first onion ring.

"What trail ride?"

"The Last Chance over on the Cottonwood. I figured you'd heard about it since you've been over there some."

The Last Chance Trail Ride. How many times had he wanted to go on that as he'd been growing up? He couldn't then, but those obstacles no longer stood in his way. He didn't even need an invitation. It was open to anyone who owned or could borrow a horse, an event to bring together the community before winter started throwing punches.

Hadn't he just told himself to leave Elly be, that it was best for everyone involved?

"Don't have a horse."

"Hello, you're in Wyoming. I think we can find you one."

Will smiled at Delia's eye rolling. "Ya think?"

"My cousin Jay has a stable between here and Markton. I'll hook you up."

Will thought about refusing, about staying away from the trail ride and Elly. But he wasn't that type of person anymore—the type who avoided things that could end up causing him pain. The plain truth was he wanted to see her, and this was the perfect opportunity. He wasn't going to let this situation with her father throw up roadblocks. If she didn't like him the way he did her, that was one thing. He'd deal. But something that was out of either of their control? That was a stupid reason to steer clear of each other.

"Sounds good."

"I'll give him a call and see what he's got available." Delia took her onion rings and headed back out to her desk.

Will imagined what Elly's face would look like when she saw him astride a horse. No more allergic, nerdy Billy the Kid. He was a man who wanted a woman, and damn if he wasn't going to figure out how to let her know it.

Delia paused in her exit and spun back toward him. "Oh, I forgot to tell you. Someone named Kate Sturgeon called first thing this morning. She didn't want to leave a message, but she said she'd call back."

"Okay." Will deliberately didn't meet Delia's eyes, didn't want her seeing more than he cared to reveal.

Kate was beautiful, smart, fun, and she was going to be a talented attorney. She'd make someone a great girlfriend. She just couldn't be his anymore.

SCATTERED SNOW FLURRIES drifted through the cold air as Elly maneuvered Jasmine among the dozens of people and horses congregated along the edge of the Greybull River. She'd had a good morning workout with Pepper, who was enjoying a well-earned rest. Plus, this close to Denver and hopefully the Finals, she didn't want to risk her getting injured out on the uneven, frosty ground.

"Looks like a good turnout," said Maryanne, Dusty's fiancée, as she eased up alongside Elly on Snowball. Even after a few months on the ranch, Maryanne still wasn't comfortable on horses. The old mare was even a stretch.

Elly laughed when she looked at Maryanne.

"What?"

"You should see your nose. You look like Rudolph."

"Hey, I'm outside and haven't frozen stiff yet. I'd say that's an accomplishment."

"True." Maryanne hadn't fled back to L.A. as the temperature had started to dip, earning her respect from the entire Cody clan. "There's Dusty. Maybe he'll keep you warm."

Maryanne waggled her eyebrows before gently nudging her horse forward. "I like how you think."

Elly chuckled. But the chuckle faded when she scanned the crowd and saw all the happy couples. Walker and Paula chatting with friends. Dex and Josie sitting on the tailgate of Dex's truck since he still couldn't ride after blowing out his knee. Dusty and Maryanne looking all googly-eyed at each other. Even Elly's parents sat side by side astride their mounts. She tried not to think about how it might just be for show, to keep the gossip at a minimum. Because Elly suspected people were talking. At the very least, the rest of her brothers and their better halves had found out. Things had been really strained the past couple of days with no one coming right out and talking about it but doing a lot of avoiding of the subject and their father.

But the situation with her father and Mark wasn't what was weighing down her heart right now. It was an unfamiliar loneliness born of watching the glances and loving touches between the couples. She felt alone in a sea of people. For the first time in her memory, she didn't even have Janie to talk to during the trail ride.

They still hadn't talked, and Elly wasn't sure how she felt about Janie keeping secrets from her. On one hand, had she done any better when she'd found out about the affair and hadn't talked to Janie about it? On the other, Janie had known for months—months in which they'd spent a lot of time together. Whether or not she was being fair to Janie, she was still hurt by her best friend keeping such a secret. There were too many secrets coming to light. She hated them all.

Elly stared out at the Greybull as it rolled over its rocky bed. In warmer weather, people fished it for its genetically pure Yellowstone cutthroat trout, but now it looked cold and uninviting—as if it was hurrying to reach a warmer climate. If she wasn't in the midst of make-or-break time in the rodeo season, she might be tempted to do the same.

The sound of hooves clomping up the trail from the pasture where everyone had parked their trucks and trailers drew her attention. When the man coming into view raised his head, she couldn't believe whose face she saw below a chocolate brown cowboy hat.

Will's gaze met hers and he headed straight for her. She didn't move, struck by how incredibly good he looked in faded jeans, scuffed boots and a tan ranch coat. To think he used to be a spindly boy too allergic to horses to even go near them, let alone ride. Now he looked made to ride a horse. Heaven help her, but he caused her heart to beat double time.

"Howdy, ma'am," he drawled as he tapped the front rim of his hat.

She laughed. "I've heard of cowboy poets, cowboy cooks, but never cowboy lawyers."

"I'm a man of many talents."

A flush of warmth made her resettle herself, causing Jasmine to take a side step. Elly experienced an instant conviction that Will was, indeed, good at many things. She tried not to think where some of those things might take place.

"I didn't know you were riding today," she said.

"I always wanted to do this when I was a kid. Better late than never, right?" he asked with a wink.

What was the man trying to do, make her melt? How would she explain that to everyone when it was thirty-three degrees?

As if to remind her that she wasn't in a balmy, tropical locale oozing with longing, a gust of wind laden with snowflakes chilled her cheeks and caused her to lift her collar to protect her neck.

Jesse emerged from the crowd and headed down the trail that wound along the river. Other riders fell in behind him, typically in pairs. Her heart ached for Jesse. He took so much responsibility on himself when he too was trying to concentrate on doing well in the upcoming Finals. As she watched him riding away, it struck her that she wasn't the only lonely one following the Greybull today.

"You okay?" Will asked.

But she wasn't lonely anymore, was she?

"Yeah." She guided Jasmine into the middle of the line, several people back from her mom and Anne's best friend, Edith Lancaster, and well away from her father. That left the rest of her brothers to fall in farther back. Most everyone had been on this ride before, but her family still took their responsibility for keeping everyone safe seriously since they were on Cody land.

Will guided his mount into line next to hers.

"Where'd you get the horse?" she asked.

"Framingham Stables. Delia got me a good deal."

Elly couldn't help laughing a little. "Yeah, because lawyers have to watch their pennies."

"Maybe we have other things we'd rather spend them on."

Elly looked at him and felt his words had some sort of deeper meaning, something tied to her. Either something was in the air today or she was slipping off her rocker. She didn't shake her head even though she wanted to, instead directing her gaze to the west.

"Think we'll get real snow?" Will asked.

"Nah. Mother Nature is just teasing us today."

"Just like a woman."

She eyed him. "Careful. You might find yourself taking a really cold bath in the river."

He responded with a dramatic shiver. "Then you'd have to save me."

Elly half expected him to suggest she'd have to warm him up, too, but he didn't. Probably a good thing because she wasn't entirely sure she wouldn't agree on the spot. His presence today was making her skin tingle, almost as though he was finally really focusing on her fully. That attention was so much more powerful than what he'd paid her before. Something had changed.

They rode in silence for a few minutes until they reached a wider, higher part of the trail and Will steered his gray gelding off to the side. He sat staring out across the valley, his eyes seeming to miss nothing.

Elly stopped, admired the image he made there. She pulled her camera from the bag that kept it thickly insulated against the cold. As quickly and quietly as she could, she lifted it and shot several photos before he turned in her direction. And one more even though she typically didn't take shots of people facing her. They never seemed as real or honest as profiles and silhouettes.

"With the views here, there's got to be something more interesting to take photos of," he said, a smile tugging at his lips.

Not really.

"Nobody's safe from the camera." She tried to sound

teasing, flip, and wasn't able to tell if she succeeded. She turned and took several shots of the line of people approaching where they sat and then some of those who were farther along the trail as it followed a bend in the river up ahead.

"I'd forgotten how beautiful it was here," Will said, reflecting the wonder she often felt while staring across the land, no matter how many times she'd seen it.

"Yeah. I can't imagine any place on earth being more beautiful."

He looked at her. "So during all your travels, you've never been tempted to relocate?"

"Considering what I mostly see in those places are horse barns and arenas, no."

"Good point." He smiled, making Elly focus on his lips. Would they be chilled by the snowy air or warm and welcoming?

She jerked on Jasmine's reins a little harder than necessary. "Better catch up with everyone else." By now, the entire line of riders had passed them by, leaving them to bring up the rear of the column.

"It's nice riding back here," Will said as he fell into place beside her. "Leisurely."

And she only had to hide how he was making her fidgety from him and not a bunch of neighbors who knew her perhaps too well for a mask to work.

"How are your practices going?" he asked after they'd also rounded the bend in the river.

"Well. I wish I could just go compete tomorrow instead of having to wait."

"Impatient?"

"Just ready. Waiting for something I want to do so badly is torture."

"I know the feeling."

The way he said it made her look over at him, only to find him watching her with an intensity that made her want to leap onto his horse with him, kiss him silly and then have him wrap his arms around her as they rode on.

She swallowed and searched frantically for a response. "What about you? Do any of your outdoor activities in the winter?"

"I've done some winter backpacking and camping, some skiing, but have to admit I like the other seasons much better." He looked out at the frigid surface of the river. "And I have no desire to try kayaking anywhere in the state of Wyoming until, oh, say, June."

"Wimp."

He raised his eyebrows. "Wimp, huh? How about you join me for some mountain climbing in the spring and we'll see who the wimp is."

"You're on."

The idea that spring couldn't come fast enough bounced around in her head as the string of riders crossed the river and started making its way back to the starting point.

"So, how are you liking living in Cody?" she asked.

"It's nice. More choices than Markton, obviously."

She laughed. "Hard to be less." Markton had its own

charm and would always be home, but sometimes one wanted more dining options than the Sagebrush. "You don't miss Denver?"

"Parts of it, sure. I have friends there. Would definitely be easier to make a living in a city that size. But living here has its benefits, too."

The way he looked at her made Elly think maybe she was one of the benefits in his mind. That thought caused happiness to spread through her like a warm current.

When the ride came to its conclusion and riders made for their trailers, Elly panicked. She didn't want the day to end. Well, it wasn't ending because the barn dance that always came after the ride still lay ahead, but she didn't know if Will would be there. She'd opened her mouth to ask him when Maryanne and Paula rode by.

"Elly, your friend knows about the dance, right?" Maryanne asked, a mischievous look on her face.

"Wouldn't miss it," Will said to Maryanne. When he looked back at Elly, the bright look in his eyes warmed her chilled skin.

"Guess I'll see you later, then," she said. Before she made a blithering fool of herself, she kicked Jasmine into a trot and headed for home.

It wasn't until she came within view of the homestead that she realized she'd been with Will for several hours and not once thought of Mark Hansen or Will's involvement in the situation.

Maybe she didn't have to hold herself away from what she wanted more every day after all.

THE BARN DANCE WAS BY no stretch of the imagination a formal affair. Still, Elly locked herself in her room and changed into clean jeans and a bright aqua shirt, things that didn't smell horsey. She washed her face and applied a smattering of makeup, just enough to give her pale complexion a little color.

After brushing out her hair, she considered leaving it down. But that seemed like too obvious a gesture. Sure, she wanted to figure out if Will was really interested, but she didn't want the entire barn full of people wondering what was up. After all, she hardly ever wore her hair down. So a fresh ponytail it was, even if she did use the curling iron to add a little extra femininity to the end.

She slipped a pair of silver hoop earrings in, then stood straight to examine her appearance in the mirror, wondering if Will would like what he saw.

Only one way to find out.

She heard the band begin to play as soon as she stepped outside. People were still making their way from their vehicles, and she joined the stream heading inside.

"Going to save me a dance, Elly?" Chester Goodlaw asked her as she walked in next to him.

Chester, who was eighty if he was a day, was nonetheless as cute as he could be.

"I always save room on my dance card just for you." Elly leaned over and kissed him on his cheek, weathered from many decades of riding the range in all kinds of Wyoming weather. Chester's family, like her own, had been in Wyoming since the territory had more Shoshone residents than white settlers.

Elly adopted a casual demeanor as she made her way through the crowd, chatting with neighbors and accepting good wishes for her upcoming ride in Denver. When she arrived at the refreshment table, her mom poured her a cup of punch.

"You look pretty, dear."

Elly shrugged. "Just cleaned up a little."

"Wouldn't have anything to do with a certain young man, would it?"

Elly took a drink while she tried to come up with a response.

Anne laughed, and the sound lifted Elly's heart. It amazed her that her mom could still find joy in teasing her about a man when her own husband's actions should have destroyed any belief she'd ever had in romance.

"Have to say that boy grew up very nicely," Anne said.

Elly decided not to deny it and said, "Yeah."

"Go ask him to dance." Anne pointed toward the far corner of the barn. "He's back there talking to your brother."

Elly spotted Will with Jesse and her heart dropped. Surely they weren't discussing the case here, among all these people.

"Go on," her mom urged.

Elly gulped down the rest of her punch and placed the empty cup on the table. "I owe Chester a dance first."

Without waiting for her mom to say anything else, she started weaving her way through the guests.

Instead of making her way to Chester, however, she edged along the back of the crowd surrounding the dance floor, not making eye contact with anyone. She wasn't in the mood for small talk. Laughter, music and the thump of boots on the wooden dance floor that had been pulled together for the occasion filled the barn.

Elly found a less populated spot and leaned against the wall. She watched as the couples spun around and two-stepped like pros to the band's enthusiastic playing of new and classic country tunes. She wanted to be among them—with Will.

She couldn't see him and Jesse from where she now stood, and maybe that was best. The pang of loneliness she'd experienced before the trail ride swamped her again. Not just for a man, but for the life she'd led before her world had tilted on its axis. And for Janie. Her absence weighed heavier now than it had even on the trail ride. Everything was just…wrong. And Elly was left feeling like she was grasping for something, anything to hold on to.

"May I have this dance?"

She almost thought she'd imagined the request, but when she looked to her side, there stood Will with his hand out, waiting for hers. The oddest sensation of being a princess at a ball enveloped her as she placed her hand in Will's and let him lead her into the whirl of dancers.

"So, lawyers dance, too?" she teased.

He leaned close to her ear. "Men dance when there are pretty women to dance with."

Elly loved the delicious warmth those words sent through her.

Will proved to be a good dancer, which made him even sexier. Even if he'd been atrocious, Elly didn't think she'd care. Just being this close to him and having him touching her was enough.

No, it wasn't enough. But she wasn't going to demand or hope for anything more because fate might decide she was greedy and take away this bright spot in her life.

One song led into another, and Will didn't show any sign of freeing her for any other partners. Her heart swelled at the same time her commonsense brain was telling her not to read too much into the situation.

After one song ended, Chester pecked on Will's shoulder. "Hey, pup. You're hogging the prettiest girl in the place, and this little lady owes me a dance."

Will handed her off to Chester with a smile and a wink for her.

"Got it bad, do ya?" Chester asked as she watched Will pair up with Delia.

Elly returned her attention to her dance partner. "Just being neighborly," she said in a halfhearted attempt at denial.

"Uh-huh. My eyes ain't that bad yet."

Elly realized Chester wasn't the only one who'd noticed when she glanced toward Will. Delia played at wrapping her leg around him then laughed her infectious laugh.

Elly's brothers didn't look as amused. Walker, a veteran of the war in Iraq, stared at Will like he wanted to toss him in a dungeon and try some interrogation tactics on him. Dex and Dusty just looked as if they wanted to put the fear of God in him. She didn't dare try to find Jesse in the crowd.

They all made her want to scream. When the song ended, she thanked Chester for the dance then made her way toward Will, not caring what anyone thought. She was an adult, and she could dance with whomever she wanted to.

"I kept him warm for you," Delia said as she backed away from her boss.

Heat suffused Elly's cheeks.

"I'm going to dock your check for being ornery," Will said.

"No, you won't." With a little wave, Delia sashayed her way through the crowd, her shiny, deep-red bob swaying.

The band struck up a slow song, and Will wasted no time pulling Elly into his arms, close. He was indeed warm, causing her to want to wrap herself in him. He smelled so deliciously male—musky, simple with a hint of the Wyoming outdoors. She found herself stepping even closer, inhaling, nearly laying her cheek against the fabric of his cream-colored shirt.

She closed her eyes and let him lead her, focused on the feel of his larger, calloused hand clasping hers, felt his breath atop her head.

She caught her brothers' stares a couple more times,

including the dark look on Jesse's face. But Will seemed oblivious. That or he just didn't care. That possibility caused a ridiculous amount of happiness to well up inside her—a welcome sensation since so much of her life was turned upside down.

Toward the end of the dance, Will leaned close to her ear. "Can I walk you back to the house?"

She glanced up at him and nodded. He guided her off the dance floor, stopping a couple of times to talk to people he hadn't seen in years. When she saw him do a casual scan of the crowd before urging her toward the exit, she realized he hadn't been as unaware of her brothers' stares as he'd made it appear. When she glanced back, the crowd blocked them from anyone with the last name Cody.

Oh, Will was good.

She giggled. Slipping away like that felt naughty, and she liked it.

The coldness of the clear night soaked in as soon as they stepped outside, and the frost crunched beneath their boots. Everyone would be scraping their windshields before they could head home. Despite the chill, Elly warmed when Will slipped her hand into the crook of his arm and placed his large hand atop her smaller one.

"Think that will go down in the annals of great escapes?" he asked.

She laughed. "Right up there with Houdini."

When they reached the front steps of the house, Elly

climbed two until Will tugged back on her hand, halting her so that she was almost eye level with him.

"I had a nice time tonight. Today, too." His voice was low, sexy. It almost caressed her, temptation itself.

"I did, too."

They stared at each other for a couple of suspended moments before Will lifted his hand and grazed her cheek with his fingertips.

"What would you say if that geeky Billy the Kid character wanted to kiss you good-night?"

A surge of undiluted adrenaline shot through her. "I don't know because I don't see him anymore."

Will's hands slid to the back of her head. She closed her eyes in anticipation as his mouth moved toward hers. His kiss, soft and firm at the same time, promised so much more. The tingling that raced through her had nothing to do with the chill in the air and everything to do with the need Will Jackson had awakened in her.

Will pulled away, leaving Elly in a daze. A beautiful daze, but a daze nonetheless.

"Will you go to dinner with me tomorrow night?"

"Yes." No hesitation. She'd go with him right now if he asked. She loved this feeling of breathlessness and warmth and yearning he brought out in her. So incredibly different from every man she'd ever dated.

She felt him smile against her lips as he moved in for another kiss. As he sent her mind spinning like a windmill in a storm again, she ran her fingers through his hair to grip the back of his head, urge him closer.

Will made a sound—part moan, part plea—and

deepened the kiss. His hands went to her back and pulled her closer. Then it was her turn to make appreciative sounds against his mouth.

When Will broke the kiss, he placed a sweet peck on her forehead. "I think I better go before your brothers get curious and come to investigate."

"They always were annoying."

He laughed and she liked how the sound rumbled in his chest.

"So, tomorrow night?" he asked.

"Sounds good."

"I'll call you."

She nodded and forced herself not to pull him back into her arms when he broke contact and headed for his vehicle out there in the sea of Fords, Chevys and Dodges. She stood on the porch, hugging herself against the cold now attacking her without Will's warmth encircling her body in a protective cocoon. Only when the taillights on his SUV faded into the night did she turn and head inside.

Her good mood dimmed when she stepped inside to find Jesse sitting on the couch. Great. He'd come in the back way. How much had he heard or seen?

He nodded toward the front door. "Do you really think that's a good idea?"

Fed up with her brothers thinking she needed bodyguards, she crossed her arms and stared at him. "Yes, as a matter of fact I do."

"What is it they say? Mixing business and pleasure is a bad idea."

"He works for you, Jesse. Not me."

He locked his eyes with hers. "He does work for you, whether you like it or not. You will be affected by the outcome of this situation as much as I will."

"What exactly is it that you think I'm going to do? Keep him from digging around in Dad's sordid past? Finding out that you're not the oldest Cody brother?"

She shouldn't have said it. The hardness in his face deepened until he looked so much like their father when he was angry that it shook her.

Elly uncrossed her arms and took a step forward. "I'm sorry. I didn't mean that. It's just…well, having you all still hovering around me like I'm a teenager gets really old. I'm a grown woman. I can make my own decisions."

"Can you? Seems like you ought to be focusing on your training and not getting sidetracked."

Her hackles rose. "Did you tell Walker that? Dex? Dusty?" She cursed and stalked several steps across the room. "You all need to back off. And if I make a mistake, then it's no one's fault but mine. I don't need you all riding in like the damn cavalry to save me and stringing up the guy."

As she said it, she couldn't imagine Will ever hurting her. Though this new, older Will was a lot different than the boy he'd once been, she'd still seen the calm, kind soul she'd always associated with him.

Maybe that's what really attracted her. He wasn't like her brothers—or her father. She loved them all, but she didn't think she wanted to end up with someone like them. She had never realized that before. Could that be why she'd never gotten serious with any of the guys on the rodeo circuit either? They were cut from the same cloth, and it had never occurred to her that it wasn't the cloth she wanted in a man.

"Fine." Jesse's single word was clipped, hard, final. "Just remember what's at stake." He stood and stalked out the back door, slamming it hard enough to rattle the windows.

She wasn't sure if he meant the state of their family's legacy or her chance at the Finals, but it didn't matter. She couldn't do anything about the situation with Mark. And she was perfectly capable of seeing Will and devoting the time needed to her training.

She ignored the tweak of doubt. Hated Jesse for causing it to bloom into existence.

With a shake of her head, she walked to her room. She had an early practice planned for the morning. But fifteen minutes later she was still sprawled across her bed, fully clothed, staring at the ceiling and thinking of Will and the way his kisses had made everything else fade away.

Including her training.

She closed her eyes and willed the doubt demon to go back to whatever black hole it had crawled out of.

Chapter Seven

Elly had lost count of how many times she'd relived kissing Will, how many times she'd compared the man he was now to the boy he'd once been and counted herself lucky he'd returned to Wyoming. What had she missed with him because she'd been too busy or blind to really get to know him in high school? She remembered what Janie had said about his youthful crush on her and tried to picture how he'd acted around her when they were younger. She grasped for the details of him asking her to prom.

The scene came to her. She was upset over getting dumped mere days before her senior prom.

"I'll take you," Will had said, his voice a much younger version of its current self.

She heard her own laugh and wished she could reach back through time and take it back. But no matter how hard she tried, the words she'd said wouldn't materialize.

She'd glanced at Will and saw something in his eyes as he looked away. Only now did she realize what it had been. Hurt. Bone-deep hurt. It made her want to cry.

Elly jerked at a loud noise and realized she must have drifted off. As she blinked herself awake, it registered that the noise was the sound of raised voices. She sprang to her feet and hurried from her room, through the living room and out onto the front porch.

"This is not your business. How dare you go behind my back!" Her father's voice thundered into the night as he faced off with Jesse at the bottom of the steps, two imposing men currently sporting the attitudes of bucking bulls in the chute.

"The hell it's not my business. This affects all of us."

Elly noticed the rest of her brothers in the dim light of the house's interior fixtures.

"You will put a stop to this investigation this instant."

"No, I won't." Jesse wasn't backing down—the first time he'd ever openly defied their father.

"Then I'll do it for you."

Elly couldn't tell in the half light, but she imagined her father's face was an angry red beneath his weathered tan.

"Will doesn't work for you," Jesse said. "He works for me."

"Is your sister part of the payment?"

Elly's heart froze at her father's accusation.

"She knows I think her involvement with him is a bad idea."

"*She* is right here," Elly said, barely hanging on to

the explosion of anger building inside her. "And I'm perfectly capable of speaking for myself."

J.W. turned his harsh gaze toward her, and for a moment she was a child on the verge of punishment for some misdeed again.

"Did you know about this, too?"

Elly dug her fingernails into her palms as she stared back at him, remembering she was a grown woman and not subject to his punishment anymore. That he was the cause of this entire situation. "Yes."

Her father cursed. "Betrayed by my own children."

The steam finally blew out Elly's ears. "You betrayed us first. Worse, you betrayed Mom."

J.W. stopped his bullish pacing and stared at her—not with anger but with a pain she'd swear mirrored her own. In that moment, she missed her dad as if he'd been gone for a year. But she wasn't ready to forgive—not yet, if ever.

No one spoke. They didn't even move as their father turned slowly and headed away from the homestead. The night had gobbled him up before anyone dared to take a breath.

"Elly—" Jesse began.

She held her palm out toward him. "Don't. I've heard all I can handle tonight. Just leave me alone." She denied the desire to walk off into the inky night herself and went back inside, to her room. She curled up in the bed without even changing into her pajamas, wrapped herself in her comforter, and tried to refocus on Will's kisses.

But all the reasons she shouldn't be starting a relationship right now, especially with him, kept intruding.

WILL COULDN'T STOP SMILING. He'd finally kissed Elly Cody, and it had been every bit as hot as he'd believed it would be. It had taken him forever to come down from his high the night before and go to sleep.

He stepped out of his house into what he was sure was the most beautiful day ever to dawn. Not even the frosty air could dim his mood. Though as he walked the three blocks to his office, he fantasized about spring and taking Elly climbing in the surrounding mountains, imagined her face lit up with excitement as they kayaked the Snake River. Maybe they could even go backcountry hiking and camping in Yellowstone, far away from the eagle eyes of her brothers.

Could he wait that long?

No matter what happened with the situation involving her father, he wasn't going to let it stand in the way of his and Elly's budding relationship. He'd waited for this too long to have another person's mistake torpedo his dream come true. He hadn't admitted it to himself, but deep down this was one of the reasons he'd come home—to see if the man he'd become stood a chance with Elly or if he had to put away that fantasy for good.

Delia gave him a knowing smile when he walked in the front door.

"I'm still deciding how much to dock you," he said as he walked by her toward his office.

"A happy man doesn't dock his hardworking secretary's check."

She had a point.

When he sank into his chair, he noticed Delia leaning against the doorframe.

"So? Dish. What happened after you and Elly snuck out the back?"

"We didn't sneak."

Delia waved her hand in a dismissive gesture. "Semantics. Romance under the stars?"

Will rolled his eyes. "You do realize I'm not a girl, right?"

"I noticed. And so did Elly." She waggled her eyebrows.

Will motioned toward the outer office. "Don't you have something to do?"

Delia pouted. "Party pooper. You're no fun." She spun and retreated toward her desk.

"I'm your boss. I'm not supposed to be fun."

He laughed when he heard her grumble some unintelligible response.

A few minutes later, Delia came in and dropped the day's mail on his desk. "Your mail, sir."

"Sir? Really? Just because I don't kiss and tell?"

Delia's eyes widened. "I knew it!"

Will sighed.

Though she was still smiling, Delia's tone dropped the teasing when she said, "I'm glad."

Will stared at her for a moment, waiting for a punchline, but one never came. "Thanks. Me, too."

"So, you two going out?"

"This for the local gossip mill?"

"I wouldn't call it a mill exactly. A few close friends perhaps."

"Which means all of Park County. Honestly, I don't know how you haven't put the *Enterprise* out of business."

Delia scrunched her nose at him, but he could tell she wanted to stick out her tongue. "It's a good thing I like you and think the two of you make a good pair."

"You do?"

"Well, duh. I wouldn't be curious otherwise. I know you've liked her forever. And, no, you weren't good at hiding it in high school. I think everyone knew but her."

"Nice to know I'm so obvious. That'll do wonders for my law career."

"Ah, you're not so moony-eyed anymore. I mean, anyone with eyes would have known how you felt last night, but you weren't so woe-is-me about it."

Will crossed his arms. "I was never 'woe is me.'"

"Whatever you've got to tell yourself."

Now it was his turn to feel like sticking his tongue out.

"Doesn't matter anymore," Delia said. "You grew up well, and now Elly's not so blind. You weren't the only one looking like you two were the last two people on the dance floor."

Delia's observation made excitement surge through him.

As Delia retreated toward her desk again, she said,

"Take flowers when you go to pick her up for your date. I hear girls like that."

Will smiled and shook his head. Life wouldn't be anywhere near as entertaining with anyone else manning his front office. Delia told it like it was, and he enjoyed that about her. He didn't even mind her gossip. Let the entire state of Wyoming know how he felt about Elly. Now that he'd decided to give it a second chance, he liked the idea of yelling it from the top of Grand Teton himself.

He worked on finishing the last of the paperwork on one of his other cases. Determined not to let anything dampen his good mood, he did his best not to think about how wrapping up the case would drop him back down to two.

His cell phone rang, and the display revealed a familiar number. Kate. Nothing she'd done or said made him feel like he could keep avoiding her, so he answered the call on its third ring.

"Hey, Kate."

"Will, I was beginning to think a bear had eaten you or something."

"Nah. They're too busy sleeping this time of year."

She laughed that musical laugh of hers that turned male heads for blocks in all directions. It had turned his once upon a time, had even made him think he could get past his crazy longing for a girl he'd loved when he was not much more than a boy.

"So, tired of your small-town life yet? Ready to come back and help me take the Denver courts by storm?"

He admired her persistence. She even managed not to sound needy or clingy when asking him to come back.

"Afraid not. I guess I'm just a country boy at heart."

"Pity that."

He could imagine her little pout and it had probably gotten her everything she'd ever wanted in her life. Except him.

But, really, she probably didn't want him as much as she thought she did. If he had to bet, he'd say that it wouldn't take long for her to attract another man who'd make her forget him, a guy who'd be more than happy to live his life alongside her in Denver.

One whose heart didn't still belong to someone else.

"How are things going at work?" he asked.

"Great. We just landed a big mineral rights case."

He was sure it was a lucrative case, but it held no appeal for him whatsoever.

"Sounds like you'll be busy."

"Probably. But if you wanted to come visit, I'd make the time for you."

He had to smile a little. She was going to earn a reputation as one of the most dogged attorneys in Denver. "I'll keep that in mind."

Will noticed Delia glance in his open office door as she walked toward the fax machine. "I hate to run, but duty calls."

"Okay, if you must." She paused for a moment. "I really hope it's going well. You deserve it."

"Thanks, Kate. Good luck with your case."

He hung up and ran his hand over his face. Just what he didn't need today—reminders of yet something else Elly didn't know about and the fact that he still might not be worthy of her. He'd be a much wealthier man if he practiced in the city, but then he wouldn't be with her. Elly might want to travel, but he couldn't imagine her ever being a city dweller. This land was too much a part of her, and she of it.

By the time lunch came around, he could barely sit still. He had to get outside, walk off some of his excess energy. As he grabbed his coat, a destination came to mind—Blooms and Petals for Elly's flowers.

And he knew exactly what he wanted to get.

ELLY STOMPED IN THE BACK door after her worst practice in months. From the look on Jesse's face when she'd passed him outside, his hadn't gone much better. They both had to pull themselves together, or they were going to lose their chance to win national titles this year.

She chugged a huge cup of coffee and went to the office to work. But as the day wore on, she kept thinking about how many barrels she'd knocked over, how the single-mindedness she shared with Pepper had taken an ill-timed hiatus. Elly's mind was just too cluttered with other things.

The hours continued to tick away, and still no call

from Will. Had her father made good on his threat and contacted him? Had he scared Will away somehow?

Didn't matter. She should cancel their date anyway. As much as it chapped her to admit it, maybe Jesse was right. Maybe she didn't have the capacity to focus on romance and racing at the same time.

The ringing of the phone invaded her thoughts, and she knew who it would be before answering. She took a deep breath and prepared herself for what had to be done.

"Cottonwood Ranch."

"Hey." Oh, how good his voice sounded, as decadent as a chocolate fountain.

"Hey."

"What's wrong?" he asked, surprising her.

"How do you know something is wrong?"

"Your tone of voice. You sound like a different person this morning."

She closed her eyes and leaned back in the chair, making it squeak. "I bet you're good in the courtroom."

"I hope to hold my own. Now, what's bothering you?"

Instead of breaking off their date, she launched into the details of her altercation with Jesse and then the argument involving her father. It relieved some of the pressure in her chest to let it all flow out. She wasn't used to keeping her emotions bottled up inside. She'd never realized how much she depended on Janie being in her life until she wasn't there.

"And to top it all off, I had my worst practice in ages today. If I ride like that in Denver, I can kiss the Finals goodbye."

"One bad practice doesn't spell doom."

"No, but it tells me I need to focus more." She paused, hating the next words before they formed. "I don't think now is the best time for me to be splitting my attention."

"Before you finish by canceling our date, let me ask you this—if we don't go out, will all the other things bothering you disappear?"

"No."

"So you'll be left with negative things to distract you instead of something fun."

She hadn't thought of it that way. Still, he was a distraction, albeit a very fine-looking one.

"I can't do anything about what's going on with Dad and Jesse."

"But you can avoid me."

"Will, don't make this harder than it is."

"If it's hard, sounds like you don't want to do it."

Of course, she didn't. She leaned forward, propped her elbow on the desk, and dropped her forehead into her palm.

"I'll make you a deal," he said. "One dinner. And if you still want me to back off afterward, I will. No pressure, no arguments."

It was a kind offer so typical of him, but the idea of him walking away made her heart ache.

"Okay."

"I'll pick you up at six."

When he hung up, probably to avoid her possibly changing her mind yet again, she eyed the clock. Three hours until she got to look into Will's eyes again. If she could go back and tell her teenage self that Will Jackson would one day have this kind of effect on her, she wouldn't have believed it.

Her energy renewed, she got more work done in the next hour and a half than she had the entire rest of the day put together. When she shut down the computer, she let thoughts of work, of racing times, of the simmering anger inhabiting her family fade away and went to her room to get ready for her date.

Nothing was going to stop her. Not her brothers, not her own second-guessing. Will was right. She wanted this. And it thrilled her that he evidently did, too.

WILL FOUGHT THE KIND of jitters he hadn't experienced in years as he drove up the long ranch road leading to Elly's house. Considering how easy it'd been to be with her on the trail ride and during the barn dance, the sudden attack of the nerves surprised him. They yanked him back to the days when he'd not had the confidence to approach her with more than casual friendship. Maybe the nerves had made an appearance because he knew how close she'd been to canceling this date, that she still might, and remembered how hard it was to hear her say no to his advances.

When the house came into view, he straightened and told the anxiety to get lost. He had no room for it in his life anymore. Elly had probably dated a lot of confident guys—there weren't a lot of wusses on the rodeo circuit—and he didn't want to pale in comparison.

Anticipation accompanied him to the front door along with the big bouquet in his right hand. But when Elly opened the door, whatever he'd been planning to say took a bullet train right out of his mind.

She wore a bright pink top, gray slacks that seemed to shine when she moved, and her long, blond hair fell loose around her shoulders. He couldn't recall ever seeing it down, and no wonder. Any man within view of her would cease being able to function normally.

"Hey, lose your voice on the way over?" she asked.

"You look beautiful."

Her cheeks pinkened, and he smiled that his words had done that.

"Thanks."

Another cog turned in his brain, and he lifted the bouquet of every kind of red flower the florist had been able to pull together. "For you."

"Oh, they're beautiful. Red is my favorite color."

"I know." Perhaps that was too telling, but he didn't care.

"You do?"

"I read interviews now and then."

"Rodeo magazines?"

He nodded. He'd tried to avoid them, but every once in a while he'd caved.

"Shut the door. You're letting all the heat out," Jesse said from somewhere behind her.

For a moment, her face tensed and her eyes darkened, but she appeared to let the frustration dissolve as quickly as it had formed. "Let me put these in water, and I'll be right out."

Will stood on the edge of the porch and looked up at the massive blanket of stars stretching across the wide, black sky. This really was a slice of heaven, and not just because Elly inhabited it.

She hurried out the door, now wearing a black coat. "Okay, I'm ready."

As they walked toward the Yukon, he sensed a tenseness in her and wondered what her brother had said while she was inside. To alleviate the tension, he asked, "So, how many red shirts do you have anyway?"

She chuckled. "Honestly, I've lost count. It's become a running joke, and I get them for birthdays, Christmas, you name it."

"Well, it looks good on you."

She glanced sideways at him. "Thank you."

Once they were seated in his SUV, he started the engine and then entwined his fingers with hers as naturally as if he'd been doing it for years. She didn't seem to mind. In fact, she settled back in her seat and let out a contented sigh that made him feel very good about himself.

They rode in a comfortable silence for a few minutes, until they were out on the highway to Markton. They passed the property where he'd grown up, where he'd too often felt inadequate and unable to live up to his father's expectations. He hadn't been back to the house since his mom had moved into the duplex in town. It was easier for her to care for, and she had Judith in the unit next door. It'd been two years since his father's death from heart disease, and he was glad his mom wasn't living out on the small ranch alone.

"I'm glad you talked me out of canceling tonight," Elly said.

He squeezed her hand gently. "Me, too. Otherwise, I'd be eating something I cooked, and let's just say I'm not getting a chef job at a five-star restaurant anytime soon."

"Well, I don't know if I can go out with a man who can't cook."

He smiled. "Too late."

As they rolled into town, he noticed her eyes go to the Feed and Grain. To draw her attention away from her strained relationship with Janie, he turned into a parking spot next to the Sagebrush Diner at the first opportunity.

"Looks busy tonight," he said.

"Always is. Not a lot of culinary choices in Markton."

"Guess we're lucky the food's good."

Every pair of eyes in the place turned their way when he escorted her in the front door, his palm against the small of her back. He leaned down to whisper to her.

"You think Hoyt got the word out with a special edition?"

She covered her mouth when she started to laugh. "Slow news day."

Hoyt Collins, who currently sat in a corner booth, was the one-man show at the *Markton Messenger,* a one-page, two-sided roundup of local news printed on his own laser printer and placed in stacks on the counters of all the town's businesses each Wednesday. It was as much gossip as it was actual news, but everyone seemed to gobble them up before the paper cooled.

After they were seated and had ordered, the interest from their neighbors grew less overt but was still very much there.

"Now I know what baby pandas feel like at the zoo." Elly pantomimed people pressing their faces and hands up against glass, seeking a closer look.

"Well, I hope my steak doesn't end up being bamboo shoots."

"What, going off to the city didn't turn you into a vegetarian?"

"I'm not that much different than I used to be."

"Oh, yeah, you are. In a good way."

Will's pulse leaped at her words, at the appreciative tone.

They spent a few minutes talking about a couple of cases he'd worked on in law school, then about her time at college.

"Did you ever think about not coming back here?" he asked.

"No. Though lately I've been wondering about the wisdom of that decision."

"I know this sounds like a platitude, but this will pass."

"I don't see how it can." Her shoulders slumped as she stared down at the table.

He tried to divert her away from her train of thought. "But you like what you do for the ranch?"

Elly looked up again. "I do. And it works well with my training schedule."

"Do you think you'll keep competing after winning the Finals?"

She fiddled with the salt shaker, which was shaped like a cowboy boot. "You're assuming I'll win the Finals. I might not even make it that far."

"You will."

"What makes you say that?"

"Call it gut instinct."

"Well, I like how your gut thinks." She smiled, which always caused a warm, wonderful feeling to envelope him.

One subject of conversation led effortlessly into another as they ate their dinner. Will hated the idea that he would have missed this if he hadn't talked her out of canceling, if he hadn't decided to give a relationship with her a second, grown-up chance.

"Do you remember the time Delia nabbed Mr. Childers's favorite sweater from his classroom and replaced the flag in the front of the school with it?" he asked.

Elly, in mid-drink, nearly choked. "I remember how purple his face turned."

"She was trying to figure out if it was just one sweater or if he had an entire closet full of the things."

"She is a sneaky little woman," Elly said. "Funny, but sneaky. I think it's cool she's working in your office."

"Never a dull moment."

Elly opened her mouth to say something else but froze. Her gaze was directed behind him.

When he looked, he saw the equally stunned look on Janie's face. And the stress on Mark Hansen's. Will might have imagined the suspended conversation around them, but he didn't think so. In that moment, he realized that word of what was going on with the Codys and the Hansens had somehow gotten out.

Not all the stares when they'd entered the Sagebrush had been because of speculation about their romantic relationship.

Elly reached out and started to say something, but Janie broke eye contact and headed toward the other side of the restaurant. The centrally located bar would block her and Mark from Elly and Will.

The sound of Elly's fork hitting her plate brought his attention back to her. He could almost see the shield going up around her, protecting her from the pressing attention of those around them.

He slipped enough cash from his wallet to pay for the meal and a generous tip, then took her hand. "How about we have something your mom made for dessert?"

She didn't answer or nod, just allowed him to lead her out of the restaurant.

He wanted to kick himself for not taking her to Cody, or maybe even to Sheridan for their night out. Not a place where every living soul knew everything about her from the day she was born into the area's most prominent family.

"I'm sorry," he said when they reached his vehicle.

"Not your fault." She sounded so distant, like she'd turned a switch on her feelings to the off position.

He touched her shoulder, turned her so that she faced him. When he saw her chin quiver, he pulled her close, wrapped his arms around her and kissed the top of her head. He wanted nothing more than to have her in his arms forever.

But not like this.

Chapter Eight

When Will's strong arms wrapped around her, shielding her from the rest of the world, Elly thought she might love him. She couldn't imagine being held by anyone else who could make her feel like life wasn't falling down around her. She never wanted him to let her go.

But he had to, of course. They couldn't very well stand outside the Sagebrush all night. Not that the tongues could wag any more than they already were. What had she been thinking when she'd said the Sagebrush was fine? Hell, it was right across the street from where Janie worked.

Though she didn't want to, she stepped back from Will. "Let's go."

He didn't grill her with inane questions like, "Are you okay?" He knew she wasn't and didn't manufacture stupid conversation to fill the silence.

As he drove her home, she stared out into the surrounding darkness.

"If you want to talk about anything, I'll listen," he said.

She didn't respond at first, but something deep inside

her told Elly that if she unburdened herself, her chest might not hurt so much.

"I just keep thinking about the look on Janie's face."

"She was surprised. You both were."

"It was more than surprise. It was like…I'd stabbed her in the heart or something. I'm not the one who kept the secret for months."

"No. But I'm guessing she knows what I'm doing and seeing you with me has her questioning everything."

"Questioning our friendship? We've been like sisters."

Will reached over and took her hand in his, squeezed it. "I think she's in probably as much shock about the situation as you are. She thought Mark was her full brother almost her entire life. And he's the only sibling she has."

"He might be her full brother."

"He might." But Will didn't sound like he believed it.

She turned toward him, watched his face in the dim glow of the dashboard lights. "Have you found out something?"

"No." He didn't elaborate, and she wasn't in the frame of mind to push, afraid of what she'd hear if she kept picking at the scab.

She went back to watching the darkness outside and tried to put herself in Janie's shoes. How would she feel if she suddenly found out one of her brothers wasn't wholly hers, that he was Tomas Hansen's son? Would she have been able to tell Janie, or would she have borne the horrible, painful secret alone, hoping it never came to light? Would she keep quiet for fear she'd lose her brother to the Hansen family?

Janie and Mark had always been close, and she knew Janie well enough to know this had to be hurting her, scaring her.

"You'll work it out," Will said. "It might take some time, but you and Janie have been best friends too long for that to all go away."

"I hope you're right."

"I usually am."

Now the low light revealed the barely contained smile on his face.

"I see you picked up an ego somewhere along the way."

He glanced at her and winked. "Not ego if it's true, sweetheart," he said in a truly bad Humphrey Bogart imitation.

"Tell me again why I went out with you."

"Because I'm irresistibly good-looking and charming?"

She snorted, but inside she couldn't agree more. It was a minor miracle she'd gone from heartbroken to laughing in the space of a few miles, but she had—thanks to him.

When he pulled up next to the house and shut off the engine, he hopped out and came around to her side of the vehicle. She was all for women doing things for themselves, but she still sat until he opened the door for her. She didn't think a little chivalry spelled the death of female empowerment. Sometimes it was just nice.

They walked in together as if it were the most natural thing to do, and Elly was glad to see Jesse wasn't at home.

"So, would you like German chocolate cake, orange-cranberry scones or key lime pie?"

"Have you opened a Cottonwood Bakery, too?"

She moved toward the coffeemaker. "It's Mom. Baking is her coping mechanism when she's upset."

"Oh, sorry."

"It's okay."

"Though compared to some coping methods I've seen people use, baking is a good one."

"Yeah, but we all get fat." She set the coffee to brewing. "So, which one?"

"Cake sounds good."

Elly sliced two pieces as Will wandered around the room. She glanced at him when he stopped in front of the floor-to-ceiling bookshelf.

"Lot of travel books. Have you been to these places?"

"Only a couple." She poured two cups of coffee and placed them beside the cake slices on the table.

"Then you have a poorly concealed guidebook fetish?"

She smiled. "Perhaps." She slid into her chair, and Will followed by sitting across from her. "Running the Web site and blog for the ranch has allowed me to get to know people around the world. People who just like to read about the daily activities here, ones who have visited, ones who plan to visit. Even a couple of writers who come to me with research questions about ranching and Wyoming in general. I get interested in where they're from and buy travel books."

"So, do you want to visit all those places? Rome. Argentina. Pennsylvania's Amish country?" He said the last with a smile, a nod to how different it was from the other two.

"Sure, someday maybe."

"After the Finals, you should travel some."

"I'll be busy." She took a bite of her cake and savored the taste.

"Are you ever not busy?"

She thought about it. If she wasn't training, she was working on the Web site or blog. If she wasn't doing that, she was conducting tours or working on other PR projects for the ranch. And if she didn't make the Finals this year, she knew she'd craft a more ambitious training schedule for next year.

"That's what I thought," Will said, then took a bite of his own slice of cake.

"I'll travel someday. It's just more of a fantasy than reality now."

"You like the photography too, right?"

The change in conversation direction caused her to pause raising another bite of cake to her mouth. "Yeah."

"Why?"

"It's relaxing, creative."

He nodded toward the shelf of guidebooks. "Think of all the photos you could take around the world."

It stunned her that she hadn't thought of that. But her photography had always been tied to the ranch—just like everything else in her life. And she'd never minded. She loved it here. Still, the idea of photographing the rest of the world held definite allure.

"Just because something is fantasy doesn't mean it can't become reality," he said.

When she met his gaze, she thought he was talking about a lot more than world travels.

Jesse walked in the front door, intruding on the moment. "Will." He obviously still didn't approve of the personal nature of her relationship with Will, but to his credit he didn't verbalize it. Still, Will had to know because he shifted in his seat in a way that signaled he was going to leave. At that moment, she wished she didn't share a home with her brother.

Jesse went into his office but didn't close the door.

"I better go," Will said.

"I'll walk you out."

After they both retrieved their coats, Will clasped her hand right as they passed Jesse's office. She smiled at the deliberate gesture, and Will Jackson claimed a little more real estate in her heart.

They walked hand in hand until they reached his SUV. When she stepped into the circle of his arms, it felt as if she'd been performing the same motions for years.

"I'm sorry tonight got spoiled," he said as he ran his thumb along her cheek.

"It would have been worse if you hadn't been there." She hesitated, staring up at him for a couple of seconds before continuing. "You somehow made me feel better when I didn't think I could."

"Do my talents know no bounds?"

She laughed. "Oh, hush and kiss me already."

"Gladly."

Could there possibly be a better sensation in the universe than the tingling, warm, sweet taste of Will's lips on hers? She sank into him and let the enjoyment pour over her. When he ended the kiss, she smiled up at him and was rewarded with one of his own.

"Remember what I said." Will pushed a wisp of hair away from her cheek. "If you want something, don't let anything get in your way."

His words reverberated in her mind long after the sound of his vehicle's engine was lost in the night.

EVEN THOUGH SHE'D BEEN working toward the National Finals Rodeo for as long as she could remember, something about hearing Will say, "If you want something, don't let anything get in your way," gave her extra drive. Despite the terrible practice the day before, she approached the barn the next morning with a new outlook.

The drive and desire were still there, but she let herself remember the joy in her racing, as well. Just before mounting Pepper, she closed her eyes and thought back to when she'd just started barrel racing. She'd knocked over every barrel, but the feel of her horse's power beneath her and the wind whipping past her face had been magic.

With that thought in mind, she hopped into the saddle and shoved everything but racing her absolute best race from her mind.

When her third trip through produced her best time ever, her first thought was to call Will and tell him all about it. Not Janie. Not a member of her family. Will. She was falling for him—the most unexpected guy.

As she went through the rest of her morning, she allowed herself to think about what things she wanted beyond the Finals. If she managed to win in Vegas, would her drive to go for it again be there? She guessed she wouldn't know until, or if, it happened. But what else did she want?

She admitted she did want to travel. The desire had been there for a long time, but she'd relegated it to simmering on the back burner.

Definitely wanted to continue to spend time with Will, see where this attraction between them led.

Elly thought back to dinner the night before and realized there was one other thing she wanted—to heal her relationship with Janie. She couldn't imagine not having Janie in her life. It hurt just to think about that possibility.

Before she talked herself out of it, she picked up the phone and dialed.

"Feed and Grain," Janie answered.

"Hey."

Pause. "Hey."

"I was thinking, we haven't been on an overnight trip in a while. Can you get away Friday night?"

"Elly." The word sounded sad, resigned.

"If another day is better, I can work around your schedule."

"I don't think—"

"I miss you, Janie."

For several ticks of the clock, Janie didn't respond. Elly blinked against the tears that welled in her eyes.

"I miss you, too," Janie finally said.

"I really want to get together and talk. Please say you'll go with me."

Janie hesitated again. "Okay."

After they made plans to meet at a bed-and-breakfast near Powell, Elly immediately called Will. After Delia forwarded the call and Will answered, Elly said, "Imagine I'm kissing you right now."

"I charge extra for imaginary stuff."

She laughed. "How do you do that? Come up with those deliciously smart-aleck responses on the fly?"

"Another talent?"

Elly snorted.

"Okay, Delia's rubbing off on me. I can't help it. It's like snark disease."

"There are worse things."

"So, why so chipper? Just the sound of my voice?"

"Although that's nice, it's actually something you did."

Elly heard him shift in his chair and tried to imagine what his office looked like.

"And that was?"

"Told me to go after what I wanted. So I called Janie. We're going away on Friday for a girls' weekend."

"Good."

"So if you ever get tired of the lawyering gig, you totally have a future in counseling."

"Good to know I've got options."

Elly smiled even wider. The guy just filled her with sunshiney joy. "Well, I gotta go. Duty calls in the form of a bus of Korean tourists."

"Hey, Elly?"

"Yeah?"

Will lowered his voice. "Now imagine me kissing you."

"I heard that!" Delia said from the background.

"No, you didn't," Will responded.

"Yes, I did."

"Then you're fired."

"No, I'm not."

Elly laughed. "I'll let you get back to work."

"I'm glad you talked to Janie."

"Me, too."

After she hung up, Elly sat at the desk with a tremendous grin on her face. And fought the urge to drive to Cody and kiss Will for real.

Chapter Nine

When Elly walked up the stone pathway to the Tanner House B and B on Friday afternoon, Janie was sitting on the front porch's swing.

"That looks peaceful. Chilly, but peaceful."

"Yeah." Janie didn't quite meet her eyes.

Elly tried to calm the nerves roiling inside her. This sensation of being nervous around Janie made her feel like she'd taken a wrong turn somewhere and ended up in an alternate universe. But she did her best not to let it show. She was determined to recapture the type of relationship they'd had before either of them knew about the affair that had happened between their parents.

Instead of seating herself in the large wicker chair adjacent to the swing, Elly deliberately sank next to Janie like she'd been doing since they'd bonded over their mutual dislike of multiplication tables. Elly lifted the large brown bag in her hand.

"I brought five kinds of cookies and every Gerard Butler movie I could find." Janie had developed her crush on Gerry with *The Phantom of the Opera,* and had been completely done in when she'd watched his washboard abs in *300*.

"Bribery, huh?" The barest hint of the old Janie gave Elly hope.

"I tried looking up his phone number to see if he could join us for the weekend, but did you know they don't actually publish the numbers of famous people? The nerve!"

Janie's lips twitched.

Elly wrapped her arm around Janie's and leaned on her shoulder. She hated to change the tone of their interchange, but they couldn't keep avoiding the big issue if there was any hope for them to move beyond it.

"I felt horrible in the Sagebrush the other night."

"I'm sorry."

Elly lifted her head and turned to face Janie. "No, I don't want you to apologize. If anyone should, it's me. I'm sorry I got upset about you not telling me about… the situation. I know it must have been a hard thing to bear."

Janie nodded. "I felt like it was going to eat me alive." She paused, picked at her cuticles in a nervous habit she didn't display very often. "I found out that Mark had a different father when Dad was sick. He refused to let either of us help him, not even to donate blood. I thought that was odd and asked Mom about it. She brushed it off, saying Dad was just stubborn. It kept bugging me though, and later I found a letter Mom had sent to your dad back when she was pregnant with Mark. It was returned unopened, but…I opened it."

"What did it say?"

"Nothing specific, just that she wanted to meet to talk. But it made alarms go off in my head. I had no proof, but I just knew in my gut."

"Mark's known all this time?"

"No. I didn't tell him."

Elly looked at Janie, her confusion probably etched all over her face. "Why?"

"Dad was dying, Mom was beginning to slip more. I just couldn't handle anything else, and I didn't think Mark could either. I didn't think it was going to do anybody any good to know." Janie finally met Elly's eyes. "I swear, I didn't keep quiet to hurt anyone. Not Mark, not you."

She looked so haunted by the secret she'd kept that Elly clasped one of Janie's hands in hers. "I know."

"Mark didn't know until recently. He had a blood test done, but all it proved was that Dad was almost certainly not his biological father. He let your dad know what he suspected, but that's as far as he took it."

Elly slid back against the swing and used her foot to make it sway gently, trying to absorb the barrage of information. Several quiet moments passed in which the only sounds she heard were the squeak of the swing's chains and the wind in the surrounding pine trees.

She bit her bottom lip before speaking again. "This has been so surreal. Sometimes when I wake up in the morning, I think for a moment that I just dreamed it all."

"I wish we had."

"I feel like everything I've ever thought was real was actually a lie, like my family is being torn apart."

"That makes two of us." Janie picked at a small hole in her jeans. "Only I feel like I'm losing the only sibling I have." She didn't have to say the rest—that Elly was gaining another brother when she already had four. Just as Will had said Janie was probably feeling.

"You know Mark will never leave you, no matter who his father is. He loves you."

"So he says, but I don't know. I already feel I've lost part of him to Nicki. I mean, don't get me wrong. She's great, and she's really good for him. I've never seen him as happy as when he's with her. It's just…"

Elly squeezed Janie's arm. "Things are changing, but you'll always have Mark. And me." She hugged Janie and watched as the sun's bottom edge dipped below the horizon. As if on cue, the breeze turned colder. "Let's go inside and start a fire."

After a moment, Janie nodded.

They tossed their overnight bags in their respective rooms, then Elly started a fire while Janie put the cookies on two large plates and poured glasses of milk.

When Elly turned back toward Janie, she could tell something else was still troubling her friend. "What is it?"

"I bet Jesse hates Mark even more now, doesn't he?"

"Hate is a strong word."

"They've never been the best of the friends."

"No," Elly said as she moved toward the couch and

sank onto one of its arms. "I can't even remember why this dumb rivalry of theirs started."

Janie looked like she wanted to say something, but she remained silent.

"You know why?"

Janie lifted her gaze to Elly's. "Because Mark always felt like he had to work three times as hard to accomplish what Jesse did. It's not Jesse's fault. I think it's more a sense of inferiority on Mark's part. They were always competing, but Jesse had the better equipment, better horses."

"Mark does really well. He's just as likely to win the Finals as Jesse."

"Yes, but…it was just harder."

Elly did her best not to sound defensive when she responded. "Jesse works hard, too."

"I know that. And I think Mark does, too, though he's been loath to admit it at times, especially the way they try to mess with each other's heads at rodeos." Janie sighed and leaned against the kitchen table. "You know Mark isn't a big talker." She laughed a little. "I guess he's a lot like Jesse that way."

Elly nodded, unable to deny the similarity. She suspected that if she let herself, she'd find more.

"I'm not saying this to elicit pity. You know I hate that. But I think all Mark ever wanted was for things to not be so tough. He doesn't mind hard work, but I know he worries about Mom and her care. About me, though he shouldn't. I can take care of myself. Honestly, I'd be more worried about him if it wasn't for Nicki. And goodness knows I wasn't too easy on her when they first got involved. But even though she's been good for him, I still feel like he's walking around with a lot of self-induced pressure on his shoulders."

Elly thought the same about Jesse—only he didn't have a woman to love and be loved by. But he had lived an easier life than Mark. No one could argue that point. Having access to the Cody coffers—through blood and not charity—could make all the difference in the world to Mark and his family. Elly couldn't begrudge him that.

She stared at the top of the coffee table for a few seconds before lifting her gaze back to Janie. "As difficult as it is, I think we have to sit back and let them work it out for themselves."

Janie nodded, then brought the cookies and milk to the coffee table. "I don't know about you, but I'm up for a little escapism at the moment."

"Your wish is my command."

They sank onto the couch, and Elly held up two DVD cases. "So, *The Ugly Truth* or *Gamer?*"

"I'm more in need of some half-naked men."

Elly lowered the DVDs and cocked her head to the side. "How many times have you seen *300?*"

"Not enough."

Elly tossed the cases on the coffee table and grabbed another. "Scantily clad Spartans, it is."

Despite Janie's request for the movie, however, Elly sensed she wasn't as into it as normal, that she couldn't escape her thoughts. But she waited until Janie initiated more conversation.

"I've heard people talking in town. They're saying Jesse hired Will so Mark doesn't get his hands on Cody money."

Elly lowered her half-eaten snickerdoodle. "It's not that ugly. Jesse just takes his responsibility for our family very seriously." She paused, tried to view the situation from her brother's perspective. "And he's hurt, just like the rest of us. All these years, he's thought he was the eldest son, and now he finds out it's all been a lie."

"Mark wouldn't do that, go after your money."

"I know. But he might be entitled to it anyway."

"What has Will said?"

"I don't know. He only discusses the case with Jesse."

They watched the scene where Gerry and Lena Headey got hot and heavy before he marched off to certain death.

"So, have you kissed him yet?" Janie asked.

The question caught Elly off guard. She didn't know whether she should tell the truth, so she fell back on teasing. "Gerry? Nah, I'm more of an Eric Bana in *Troy* gal myself."

Janie swatted Elly's leg. "Will, you goofball."

Elly sat for a moment, recalling the feel of Will's lips on hers, the comforting strength of his arms wrapped around her, the subtle brush of his body against hers.

"You have, haven't you?"

Elly nodded.

"Can I say I told you so now?"

"Are you okay with that?"

Janie thought for a moment then nodded. "Yeah. I always thought he was nice. And he certainly did grow up to be easy on the eyes."

Elly bumped Janie's shoulder with her own. "Hey, get your own guy."

A look of longing, momentary but strong, passed over Janie's face.

"Hey, is there someone you like? Who is it?"

"No, there's nobody." The way she said it left Elly with the impression her friend was lying, but she didn't press her. She didn't feel like tempting their reconciliation.

But as the rest of the movie played out, she kept wondering who it could be. And why Janie hadn't confided in her—unless it was a recent development? Elly tried to push away thoughts that another secret sat lodged between them.

They ordered pizza and watched *The Ugly Truth* next. By the time they were halfway through *Dear Frankie,* the pizza and countless cookies were beginning to take a toll. Elly leaned her head against the back of the couch.

"I think I'm going to explode."

"Want me to call Will to come rub your tummy?"

Elly's mouth fell open as she stared at Janie. When she made a dive for her, Janie squealed and took off running. Elly chased her, swatting her with a decorative pillow. They ran and leaped over furniture until they tripped over each other's feet and ended up sprawled in the floor, side by side, staring up at the ceiling.

"You really like him, don't you?" Janie asked.

"Yeah." Elly didn't even try to mask the dreamy quality of her voice.

"I could tell."

"How?"

"The way you were looking at him. I've never seen you look at a guy like that."

Elly lifted the back of her hand to her forehead. "It came so out of the blue, so strong that it shocked me. He's so different than I remember him."

"People grow up. They change."

"I haven't. I'm pretty much the same now as when we were in high school."

"Beautiful, talented. What needs to be changed?"

"How I look at people maybe. I mean, I remember him being kind, even if we did tease him. But I never knew about his sense of humor, how he looks at the world, what he wanted out of life."

"Maybe he didn't either. Sometimes people have to leave home to find out who they are."

"I left, but I came back exactly the same. Ranch, photography, training. Training, ranch, photography."

"What else do you want?"

"I don't know really. Maybe more of the world than horse barns and arenas."

Janie lifted onto her elbow and looked down at Elly. "But you love racing."

"I do. Right now, I want to get to the Finals so much I

can taste it. But I won't be racing my whole life. I haven't really thought beyond it."

"But now you're beginning to?"

"Yeah."

"Is Will Jackson in the picture?"

Elly smiled at the thought of him. "I hope so."

Janie lay back down. "I feel sorry for him."

Elly turned her head to look at Janie's profile. "What?"

"The poor guy is going to be subjected to the Cody brothers gauntlet." She snorted. "And I guess now there might be five of them instead of four."

Elly stared, unsure how to respond until a laugh escaped Janie. Then they were both laughing, just like on so many other girls-only weekends.

Elly grabbed Janie's hand and squeezed it. "I can't tell you how happy I am that we're here."

"Me, too."

"Whatever happens with our families, let's swear we won't let it come between us again."

Janie made an exaggerated expression of considering the proposal. "Only if you promise to give me all the juicy details about Will. No fair leaving anything out."

Elly smiled when she thought that there might be future juicy details to spill. "Deal."

Chapter Ten

Elly expected Will to call when she got back from her trip with Janie, but Saturday night passed with no ringing of the phone. So did Sunday. By midday Monday paranoia had set in. And it affected her training.

"Focus, dang it," she said to herself as she lined up to take another run at the cloverleaf pattern around the barrels. But when she knocked over the second one, she didn't push Pepper too hard the rest of the run. To make matters worse, she spotted Jesse walking past the end of the arena with an "I told you so" look on his face.

As if he never got thrown off a bull.

Needing to get away from the ranch for a while, she called Janie and asked her to meet for lunch at the Sagebrush. When Elly arrived, she sank into the booth across from Janie.

Janie shoved her textbooks aside. "Bad practice?"

"I've had better." Elly nodded toward a biology book that looked like it weighed twenty pounds. "Sorry to interrupt your studying."

Janie waved her hand in a dismissive gesture. "My

eyes were crossing anyway. So what's really bugging you?"

"Will hasn't called in days."

"Have you called him?"

"No."

"Very modern and liberated of you."

"Whose side are you on?"

"I'm your best friend. I tell it like it is."

Elly sat back and pouted. "Why am I getting so worked up over this?"

"Because you've fallen for him."

"You can tell that, from seeing us together one time?"

Janie lifted her gaze from her cheeseburger. "And from listening to you enumerate his many wonderful attributes. And from the goofy smile you get on your face when you say his name."

"I do not."

"Sorry, toots. You do."

Elly responded by shoving two piping hot cheese fries into her mouth.

Janie leaned forward. "So, listen, I've got an idea. We're not exactly swamped at work today. How about I take the rest of the day off and we go into Cody to see the new exhibit on cowgirls?"

Elly suspected her friend had ulterior motives for taking her to Cody, but she agreed nonetheless. After all, it wasn't like she was going to comb the streets of Cody looking for Will. But if they happened to bump into each other again, she wasn't going to avoid him either.

But by the time they'd gone through the exhibit, checked on the stock of her photos at the gallery and perused some new offerings in a couple of stores without even a glimpse of Will, she'd resigned herself to the fact that she wasn't going to have any lucky encounters.

WILL LOOKED AT THE PAPERS spread across his desk and sighed. They didn't change no matter how long he stared.

The paternity test proved that Mark Hansen was, indeed, John Walker Cody's son. His firstborn son.

Jesse wasn't going to be happy.

And he feared that the news would reopen wounds for Elly, wounds that had only begun to think about healing.

Will sat back and rubbed his eyes. He still couldn't believe J. W. Cody had knocked on his front door at daybreak and handed him an envelope containing DNA testing results.

"The proof," J.W. had said.

"Why are you giving this to me?"

"The sooner Jesse gets his proof and realizes I'm not so senile that I'd hand over the ranch to Mark, the better. Mark has known for a while and made no demands."

"Why not tell Jesse yourself?"

"I'm not his favorite person at the moment."

Will imagined how Jesse might not be giving his

father any opportunities to get near enough to talk to him.

"I'm outta here," Delia said as she stood in the open doorway putting on her coat, bringing Will back to the present.

"Okay."

"Are you all right?"

Will leaned back in his chair. "Yeah, just tired."

"Then unchain yourself from that desk and go home. Better yet, go see Elly."

He nodded enough that Delia took it for agreement and left. Then he leaned forward and looked at the report again. With a shake of his head, he shoved it into the case file and locked the file in his desk. Going home sounded like a good idea. Maybe he'd call Elly because he wasn't sure he could face her right now, knowing what he did. Could he even keep the knowledge off his face? He had to until he talked to Jesse.

Damn, why couldn't he have crossed paths with Elly again without all this family drama complicating the situation?

He grabbed his coat and headed out the door. As he walked down the sidewalk, he smelled snow in the air. Out of nowhere, a memory of Elly during a snowball fight at school stopped him. She'd been beautiful with clumps of snow sticking to her blue knit cap and melting on her reddened cheeks.

Of course, she was always beautiful. Always would be.

As he started walking again, he spotted movement

on the opposite side of the street. Elly and Janie came out of Carlton's Coffee Shop, their gloved hands around large paper cups. He guessed their trip had gone well.

He sighed. Why hadn't he called her? Maybe a part of the nervous, unsure boy he'd once been had survived after all. Some irrational fear that things were going too well, that the proverbial rug was about to be ripped out from under their budding relationship, had dogged him all weekend.

After the day he'd had, he considered fleeing before Elly saw him, but he was too late. She spotted him and put out her hand to stop Janie, who looked his direction, too. He waved and crossed the street.

He nodded at the cups. "Looks like you two have the right idea."

"Yeah, when the snow starts flying, I start chugging," Janie said.

Will heard her but kept his attention on Elly. She looked awkward, like she'd been caught doing something she'd rather keep secret. He doubted it was buying coffee.

"So, how about I treat you ladies to dinner?"

"I've got to get going, but I'm sure Elly would love some dinner if you can take her home."

Will almost laughed at the expression on Elly's face as she stared at her longtime friend, like she was on the verge of throttling her.

"I think I can manage that," he said. He just had to not think about the proof of paternity sitting in his desk.

"Great. See ya later." Janie waved as she turned away without making eye contact with Elly.

When she rounded the corner, Elly continued to stare in her direction. "Well, that was subtle."

"I wonder if she's been taking lessons from Delia."

Elly laughed and finally looked up at him. "Oh, God, we can't handle two of them."

He extended his hand. "I was just heading home."

She hesitated for a moment but then placed her hand in his. He imagined he could feel her skin through both of their gloves. They crossed the street and walked the final couple of blocks to the house he rented.

Once inside, he took her coat and hung it on the coat rack next to the door. "So it looks like you and Janie made up."

"Yeah. We had a nice trip."

"Good."

Awkward silence filled the space between them.

"I'm sorry I didn't call. Can I fall back on the excuse that I'm male and therefore an idiot?"

Elly pursed her mouth, considering his suggestion. "Okay, I'm good with that."

Unable to stop himself, he slid his hand along her jaw then lowered his lips to hers for a kiss. She melted against him, the absolute best feeling in the world. After the kiss, he framed her face with his hands.

"When was the last time someone told you that you take a man's breath away?"

"Hmm, I think it was Corky Stephens, rodeo clown

at the Missoula Hoedown. But he'd knocked back a few by then."

"Well, I'm stone cold sober, and I've never seen anything more beautiful."

All teasing left her expression. She looked up at him as if stunned by the compliment. How could it surprise her? She had to know she was stunning.

And if she didn't, he was going to tell her every day until she believed it.

ELLY FEARED HER RIBCAGE might fail in its job of restraining her racing heart. Sure, other men had said she was beautiful, but she'd never felt they believed it without some ulterior motive that usually involved her pants. But when Will said it, she felt it down to the tiniest cell in her body.

She lifted her hand and placed her palm against his strong jaw, felt the hint of afternoon stubble. "And you, William Jackson, are a very handsome man."

"Who'd have ever imagined that in high school, huh?"

She continued to examine the planes of his face, the flecks of green in his warm brown eyes you could only see up close. "A diamond in the rough, that's all. You always had beautiful eyes though. I should have told you that then. Instead, I was too busy being a teasing twit."

"You were never a twit."

"I know you didn't like that Billy the Kid nickname, and yet we persisted with it."

"No, but I'm man enough to be able to look back and know I wasn't exactly a catch."

"But you were. I just didn't know it."

"Elly," he said in a disbelieving tone.

"You were always kind, Will. And that's more important than anything."

"Tactful," he said with a smile.

"I'm sorry."

"No need to apologize."

"Yes, there is," she said. "For that day when you offered to take me to prom and I laughed. That was horrible of me."

"It was a long time ago." Something in his tone told her that despite the passage of time, he still remembered what it had felt like.

"I'm surprised you want to even talk to me, but then you're a better person than I am. I would have probably sought revenge."

"Let's just forget it, okay?"

"Will you forgive me if I say that I'm glad you came back here before someone got wise and snapped you up?"

He wrapped his arms around her waist. "Perhaps. Maybe I'll think of some other requirements, as well."

Elly's mind immediately went to all kinds of delectable possibilities, some of which caused her skin to heat and tingle in anticipation.

"Yeah? Any ideas?" She moved even closer to him and ran her hands underneath his coat and over his back. Oh, he had what felt like a very nice back.

She saw the moment the desire deepened within him, felt it in the way his muscles stiffened beneath her hands. Had she pushed him too far?

Or not far enough?

Her own body itched for more. Not just for sex, but more…of something. Deeper emotions, deeper connections, deeper meaning.

"Elly." Her name came out more ragged than normal.

"Yes?"

"I think we better get some dinner."

As she looked up at him, her heart expanded enough to envelop him. She looked over the edge of the cliff, opened her arms wide as wings, and jumped.

"I don't."

She could almost see the question marks dancing across his eyes. In answer, she started walking backward, pulling him with her.

Halfway across the living room, he pulled her mouth to his and kissed her with such power that she felt like her muscles and bones had turned to liquid. He must have sensed her waning ability to stand—Will lifted her in his arms as if she weighed no more than a newborn chick and carried her down the hallway, into his darkened bedroom.

He didn't pause to ask if this was what she really wanted. That much was obvious. And there was no need to ask him either. In fact, they said nothing as they kissed, shucked clothing, then kissed again before moving on to the next layer of attire. Her head was still spinning when she realized she stood naked in front of him and he was running his hands lightly over her skin like she was a goddess. She couldn't explain it any other way.

And if she was a goddess, he was no less a god. All that kayaking and mountain biking had sculpted his body into a vision that left her breathless. She wanted him wrapped around her, wanted to touch every inch of his sinewy, tanned skin.

"I won't break," she whispered.

He lifted her into the bed and followed. The procession of kisses that followed nearly drove her mad with longing. He placed them on her lips, her cheeks, earlobes, neck. When he reached her breasts, she gasped and arched into him. He groaned in a way that made her feel powerful and beautiful and like the luckiest woman in the world.

She grabbed the back of his head and pulled his lips to hers again, ran her finger through his hair and then down that marvelous back. When his chest touched hers, she moaned into his mouth. She broke the kiss and used his name as a plea against his lips.

He needed no further prompting as he joined with her with such exquisite ease it was the very definition of perfect. But as he began to move, all she could think about was moving with him, inhaling his scent, feeling the muscles in his back strain beneath her hands, reaching for the ultimate pleasure with Will, giving him the same.

When she reached her peak, she didn't hold back and

let herself enjoy it fully, didn't care how much noise she made. She was able to open her eyes in time to watch Will enjoy his own release. Tears of joy gathered in her eyes.

Will noticed them the moment he shifted to her side and pulled her close, wrapping his leg over hers. He lifted his fingertip to the corner of her eye.

"What is it? Did I hurt you?"

She ran her own fingertips over his lips. "No, I've never been better. It's just…you're the one who is beautiful, inside and out." She hesitated for a moment, but she found she didn't want to hold anything back. "I've never been happier. I don't know what I ever did to deserve you."

"I could say the same thing."

"But—"

He cut off her words by kissing her again, causing whatever she'd been about to say to sizzle and disintegrate.

"Don't analyze. Just enjoy," he said.

After a few minutes of rest, they enjoyed each other all over again.

In the afterglow of the second round of lovemaking, Will nuzzled against her temple and spoke close to her ear. "You hungry?"

"I want to say no so we can stay here like this, but I'm afraid my stomach will start growling and prove me a liar."

He kissed her temple. "You stay here."

When he left the bed, she was afforded a full view

of him, every magnificent facet. Feeling a little wicked, she whistled in appreciation.

At first, he looked surprised. Then his mouth spread into a sexy smile. "Be careful or you may never get food."

"Who needs to eat?"

He growled. "We need sustenance to keep up our strength." With an unspoken promise of more pleasure later, he disappeared down the hall.

Elly rolled onto her side and wrapped herself in a sheet. She couldn't stop smiling. What she'd told him was the absolute truth—she had never felt such intense joy in her life. She drifted on a cloud of happiness, which must have carried her to sleep because the next thing she knew Will was sitting next to her on the bed, now wearing a pair of long gym shorts, with a pizza box in front of him.

"Cody's finest dining," he said.

"And very lax on the dress code, too."

"I can put on a shirt."

Her hand shot out, as if to stay him. "Don't you dare."

He laughed and leaned forward to kiss her. "You want to sleep or eat?"

Her stomach growled. "Does that answer your question?"

He scooted into bed with her. She raised herself to a sitting position, pulling the sheet up with her.

"I'm ravenous," she said as she took the first slice of gooey pepperoni and mushroom pizza.

"You must have worked up an appetite somehow."

"I believe you had something to do with that."

"Always happy to help out."

When she smiled at him, it felt like a goofy, teenage, nothing-hidden type of smile, but she didn't care. At the moment, she couldn't imagine ever being in that position with another man again. It caused a pain in her chest to think of him with anyone else.

But how did he feel?

Will wrapped his arm around her shoulders as they ate.

She shook her head slowly. "How did you know I liked pepperoni and mushroom?" she asked after a couple of slices.

He didn't answer at first, pausing long enough to make her pull slightly away and look up at his face.

"Dex and Dusty's thirteenth birthday party," he said.

"Oh, God. The one with about thirty kinds of pizza. They both ate until they got sick."

"And of all the choices, you only ate the pepperoni and mushroom."

"How could you possibly remember that?"

"You know how." His gaze met hers and didn't waver.

Her breath caught. "When Janie told me you'd had a crush on me, I didn't believe her."

"Why not?"

"Because you never said anything. I mean other than

the prom thing. And I thought you were just being nice then because you felt bad I'd been dumped."

"I knew you wouldn't be interested."

"You don't know that."

"Come on, Elly. I was two years younger, a nerd in every aspect of the word. I couldn't even be a part of the world that meant so much to you. I felt every bit as weak and inept as my dad thought I was. Not worthy of you."

"Oh, Will." She put her half-eaten piece of pizza back, no longer hungry, and stared at the greasy stains and strips of cheese on the bottom of the box.

He lifted her chin, forcing her to look at him. "Hey, none of that. It just wasn't the right time."

"And now it is?"

He searched her eyes for a moment before answering. "I don't know. Maybe. I hope so."

"Me, too."

They kissed for several minutes before Will pulled her close and just held her. The beauty and simplicity of being held like this, of resting her head against his chest and listening to the steady rhythm of his heart struck her as perfection. No worries, no problems could touch her here in this warm, comfortable, Will-shaped cocoon.

"I always thought you got along with your dad."

"We were fine, just not super close. I know he would have been happier if I'd been able to go into rodeo, become a rancher."

Elly shook her head. "He should have been proud of who you are."

"Mom says he was, but he never told me. I think he didn't know how to talk to me. We were just too different."

"Is that why you wanted to go to college so early?"

"Partly. School was boring, too. And I had other reasons."

Elly bit her lip. Had he fled home to get away from her because she didn't notice him as he'd wanted? That made her sad in the deepest part of her heart.

"I'm sorry."

"No reason to be. College was good."

"I guess you were able to be with people more like you."

He shrugged. "Eventually. I won't lie and say it wasn't hard at first, being younger than all my classmates, not knowing anyone, but I did make some good friends after a while."

She let her curiosity get the better of her. "Girl-friends?"

"A few, later on."

"Anyone serious?"

"Not really."

Elly shifted beside him. She wasn't sure why his answer unsettled her. Maybe because it felt like there was more to the story he wasn't telling.

"Why?" he asked. "Jealous?"

"Nope."

He laughed. "I think you are. Careful, you'll make that big ego of mine swell."

She tickled his ribs. He retaliated by rolling toward

her and tickling her right back until she cried out her surrender. He stopped tickling and took up kissing instead. Elly let stories of parental expectations and old flames drift away as she focused solely on the feel of the man in her arms.

WILL HAD NEVER BEEN so scared in his life. Odd since he'd never been as happy either. But he wished he'd told Jesse about the proof of paternity before he'd made love to Elly. He wished Jesse had shared the knowledge with Elly and she'd still come to Will. But he hadn't been able to resist the look in her eyes tonight, the obvious desire mirroring his own. How many times had he dreamed of holding Elly like this?

And all those dreams had paled in comparison to the reality.

He listened to Elly's even breathing and knew without a doubt that he was in love with her, that he wanted to lie side by side with her like this every night. The fact that his taking actions out of the proper order might hurt that chance ate at him. But even if he had made a mistake, he wasn't willing to walk away. Not this time.

He just hoped that whatever was happening between them was strong enough to withstand the emotional roller coaster of the days ahead and the fact that he was going to be the bearer of a finality Elly and her brothers might not want to hear. The proof he held would erase any hope that it had all been a mistake.

She woke from her dozing and kissed his chest. That simple touch had him ready to make love to her again.

The smile on her face as she looked up at him told him she knew it, too.

He shoved away his fears. "Aren't you the temptress?"

"I do my best."

Before he had to face the reality outside this room, he allowed himself to indulge once more. He'd never had sex with a woman more than once in a night, so three times left him sated and nearly unable to move. Somehow he garnered enough energy to speak.

"I think you killed me."

She laughed as her hair, that long, gorgeous hair, fell past her ear and pooled on his chest. "Did I break poor wittle Will?"

"I thought your days of teasing me were over?"

"But you enjoy this teasing."

He smiled. "That I do." They kissed for what had to be the thousandth time that night, but it never got old or less exciting. "I guess I better find the energy to take you home before your brothers mount up a posse and come beat down my front door."

"What, you're not willing to face down an angry mob for me?"

"Perhaps when you haven't exhausted me to within an inch of my life."

As if to torture him, she rose from the bed and dressed with a lot of stretching and smoothing of fabric.

"No wonder your brothers want to keep you under lock and key. You're a danger to men everywhere."

She laughed again and sashayed toward the bathroom

with an exaggerated sway of her hips so at odds with the Elly Cody who walked around in the daylight.

By the time they headed out of Cody, he'd regained enough feeling in his extremities that he didn't think he was a danger to his fellow motorists. He didn't let go of her hand, even when it began to snow.

"Looks like this will be the first real snow of the year," he said.

"Yeah. I smelled it in the wind today."

The ground had a thin coating of white when he pulled up next to Elly's house. He had the strangest sensation that her brothers knew what he and Elly had been doing this evening, but suddenly he didn't care. She was an adult, and so was he.

He accompanied her to the front door, hating the idea of the most perfect night of his life ending. And not knowing if there would be another.

"Why don't you stay the night instead of driving back?" she said.

"I'm kind of a fan of not being shot at dawn."

She cuddled close to him. "I'll protect you."

As he looked down at her, he nearly told her he loved her. But he kept it bottled inside. He had to get his duty out of the way first so he'd be free to tell her everything she made him feel, how she'd always been the one for him and always would be. He just prayed she felt the same.

He lowered his mouth to hers and kissed her with all the love he couldn't voice, not yet.

Chapter Eleven

The next morning, Elly was a little off on her racing times, but she didn't let it bother her. She knew she and Pepper could clock better times, and she wasn't going to allow a few hundredths of a second to dim the happiness vibrating through her entire body.

Her good mood carried her through a tour with fifty third-graders and an interview with *Rodeo News,* even though she wanted to cut out on the latter when she saw Will drive up the ranch road and park by the house. By the time the reporter headed toward his truck, she was ready to bust with wanting to see Will. Somehow she managed not to run toward the house.

She barely slowed to knock the snow off her boots before hurrying in the front door. When she heard voices from the office, she hoped Jesse wasn't accosting Will about his and her relationship. She was surprised to see the office door closed. Oh, this was bad if Jesse had shut her out. Fed up with the big brothering, she knocked only briefly before entering the office.

Jesse sat at the desk poring over some sort of paperwork in front of him. Then it hit her. Will was actually here to see Jesse, not her.

"What is it?" she asked Will, not her brother.

This time Will didn't look to Jesse for permission to share with her. "The results of a DNA test your father had done—they prove he's the biological father of Mark Hansen."

She shifted her attention to Jesse. "Let me see it."

"It's real," Jesse said.

"Let me see it," she said more slowly, not brooking argument.

He handed it over. Her wonderful sense of rightness and joy shattered, fell like jagged shards of glass around her. Not because Mark was definitely her brother, but because irrefutable proof of her father's infidelity was staring up at her. When she glanced back at Will, he didn't meet her eyes.

She knew in that instant that he'd known last night, when he'd made love to her over and over again.

She tossed the proof of her father's betrayal on top of Jesse's desk and walked away from Will, out the door of the office and back into the light of a day that was gray and overcast. Appropriate. She thought of taking a ride up into the more remote parts of the ranch, but she didn't want to be anywhere near Cody land at the moment, nowhere near her father. Instead, she headed toward her truck.

The front door opened and shut behind her. "Elly, wait."

She kept walking, ignoring the sound of Will's voice. Last night, she couldn't get enough of it or him.

He caught up with her and tried to take her arm. She jerked away from him. "Don't touch me."

"Elly, don't do this."

"Don't do what, Will?"

"Push me away."

"You did that yourself by lying to me," she spat at him. "What is this, revenge for rejecting you in high school?"

"I wouldn't do that, and you know it."

"Do I?"

Will stared at her for a long moment, his lips pressed tightly together like he was trying to prevent himself from saying something. "I didn't lie."

"No, you didn't. But you kept important information from me. Haven't I had enough secrets in my life lately?"

"I was hired by Jesse. It was my duty to tell him what I found, not you."

"Well, you've told him. Job completed."

"Elly, I didn't plan for last night to happen the way it did."

"Oh, nice."

"Stop twisting my words," he said, a touch of anger in his tone. "I'm happy it did, really happy."

"But you knew I wouldn't fall into your bed if I'd known about that little piece of paper, didn't you?"

He stared at her again, and she tried not to acknowledge the hurt she saw in his eyes.

"Yes."

A lump formed in her throat. She had to get out of here before she made a fool of herself and started crying.

"Then you're just another man hiding things to get what he wants. No better than my dad."

She slid into the truck, slammed the door and took off down the ranch road as fast as she could. She held the tears at bay until she hit the highway. They accompanied her all the way out of Park County as she headed east. She didn't know where she was going, didn't care. Just as long as it was away from Will and that piece of paper that changed everything—her past, her present and her future.

WILL STOOD IN THE DRIVE and watched as Elly raced away from him. Part of him wanted to speed away, as far from Elly Cody and her sharp tongue as he could get. But damned if another part didn't want to go after her, to make her understand how much she meant to him, how paternity test results had been the furthest thing from his mind as he'd carried her to his bed the night before. But her uncharacteristically cruel words proved she wasn't in a state where she could listen now. Maybe when she calmed down.

Maybe not.

Honestly, he needed time for his anger to fade, too.

He cursed himself for doing things backward. Anger at the entire situation made him clamp his jaws and have to resist the urge to punch the door of his SUV.

And to make matters worse, he felt eyes on him. Jesse had stepped out onto the front porch and didn't look too happy. Will didn't know if it was because of Elly or the confirmation of his father's adultery, not that it mattered.

But Jesse's presence didn't feel like the only one. Will stared toward the barns though he didn't see anyone. That didn't mean they weren't hidden in shadows, cooking up a way to string him from the nearest tree for hurting Elly.

Something made him look toward the ranch office. There stood Anne Cody on the edge of the porch, staring at him. From this distance, he couldn't read her expression, but that was probably a good thing. He'd seen enough mama bears protecting their cubs to know it was time to make his own getaway.

As he drove down the ranch road, he wondered if he'd ever drive along its length again. He was done with the job he'd been hired to do, and Elly...well, he didn't know if she'd ever want to see him again.

His heart weighed like a boulder, making breathing difficult. How could he have waited this long to be with Elly only to screw it up royally?

Her words—that he was no better than her dad—kept repeating in his head until he grew sick to his stomach. Despite how unfair she'd been, he still looked for her as he drove through Markton and later Cody. But there was no sign of her. At least the sun had come out and he didn't have to worry about her getting caught in a snowstorm.

He pulled into the driveway next to his house but couldn't muster the energy to get out of the vehicle. Could he stay here if he'd lost Elly for good? Would it be better to go back to Denver and take Kate up on her offer of employment? Maybe convince his mother and aunt to move there, too? Then he'd have no reason to ever set foot in Park County, even Wyoming, again.

ELLY DROVE ALL THE WAY TO Sheridan, parked and walked the streets without any destination in mind. She just needed distance, time, nothing that reminded her of Will or her family. Time to refocus on what was important—the Finals. She couldn't believe she'd almost let her brief relationship with Will steer her off the course she'd been on for years.

A poster in a shop window caught her attention. It depicted a gorgeous beach and bright blue water and proclaimed Cancun in large, red letters. What Will had said about her traveling and taking photos all over the world tried to tempt her, but she swatted it away like the pesky fly it was. Photography was a minor part of her life, something she did when she had the time. She was a cowgirl, a member of the Cody family with all the responsibilities and expectations that encompassed. She needed to stop thinking about things that were just fantasy like becoming a world traveler.

Or being held in Will's arms again.

She walked and walked, until the cold wind whipping around the edge of buildings had slapped her cheeks to near numbness. If only it could do the same thing to her heart, deadening it to feeling until she was over Will.

Had she really said the things she had to him? Part of her knew she'd been mean, unreasonable, but she was so tired of secrets and the pain they caused.

After a couple hours of aimless wandering, she made her way back to her truck and headed home. It was time to deal with the new reality because there was no going back.

When she arrived at the turn into the ranch, she pulled over to the side of the road and took a few moments to breathe deeply, to prepare herself for whatever waited at the end of the road. The drive up to the homestead house had never seemed so long. She spotted horses being loaded, feed being transferred to the horse barn, the hands going about their late-afternoon duties. To the unknowing eye, all would seem normal.

She made her way into the house and found Jesse sitting at the kitchen table, his big hands wrapped around a mug of coffee.

"Where you been?" he asked without looking at her.

"Sheridan. Needed time to think, away from everything."

He nodded like he understood. "There's fresh coffee."

She poured herself a cup and sat across from him. The silence grated on her nerves, and it wasn't going to make the conversation any easier. "So, what does this mean?"

"That Mark has a right to some of the ranch, to everything."

As she'd anticipated. But it wasn't the family fortune that mattered so much to her. It was how the situation was going to affect her family from now on.

She'd never seen Jesse look so haggard, so bone-deep weary. Yes, he could be gruff and overbearing sometimes, but she loved him. He worked hard to keep the Cottonwood Ranch thriving while not letting his dream of winning the National Finals in bull riding slide. He'd always taken his role as firstborn very seriously. And now that had been ripped away from him.

Despite all the family on the ranch, he seemed like the loneliest person in the world. At least she'd found happiness in someone else's arms for a short time. She saw every day how happy the women in Walker's, Dex's and Dusty's lives made them, and she wanted that for Jesse.

Even if it might never be in the cards for her.

At the moment, she couldn't imagine being with anyone but Will, but couldn't face being with him either. How would she know if he were keeping something important from her? How could she ever trust him?

She refused to go through the same kind of pain her mother was experiencing.

"How much?" she asked.

Jesse looked down at his coffee, but Elly felt like he was staring beyond it. "Will said it's up to Dad and Mark to work out." He took a drink of his coffee before rising and dumping the rest down the sink.

She wondered if he'd been sitting here alone with his thoughts long enough that the coffee had grown cold.

"Jesse."

He looked back at her.

"Janie told me Mark isn't interested in the ranch. I think he probably just wanted the truth."

"Well, he got what he wanted." He grabbed his coat and headed for the door. "I've got work to do."

Work awaited her attention as well, but the walls of the house threatened to close in on her. She too pulled her coat on and followed Jesse out the door. When he stopped a few feet from the house, she redirected her gaze and saw her father talking with Mark in the lengthening shadows next to the ranch office.

The ferocity of Jesse's anger came off him like a shock wave as he spun in the opposite direction and headed for the practice arena. She hated the idea of him astride a surly bull at the moment, but there wasn't anything she could do to stop him.

As she watched her oldest brother stalk to the barn, she had never felt so powerless. When she glanced back at Mark, it struck her that in reality he was her oldest brother. Even though it might never feel like it.

FOR THE FIRST TIME EVER, Will didn't feel like going to work. He doubted he'd be terribly productive, and he sure wasn't going to want to talk to anyone. Not exactly the best way to drum up business. And if word of his and Elly's blowup hadn't reached Delia already, one look at him and she'd know something was wrong.

He lingered over his coffee, but the longer he sat and tried watching the morning news, the more a feeling of claustrophobia pressed in on him. He couldn't stay in this house all day with nothing to occupy his mind.

By the time he reached work, he was an hour late. Delia started to say something, but she didn't get it out before he stepped into the doorway of his office—and saw Kate standing inside. Tall, stylish, gorgeous Kate with her long, golden-brown hair and elegant features looked so out of place that he wondered for a moment if he wasn't really awake yet.

"Kate."

"Will!" She rushed forward and wrapped him in a hug.

He was too stunned to do anything beyond offer a feeble hug back. "What are you doing here?"

"Well, you talked about how wonderful it is here so much that I had to see for myself. I booked the cutest little cabin outside town, had breakfast in a quaint diner this morning." She smiled. "And I can see the allure of practicing here if you're keeping a banker's hours."

"I had something to do this morning before coming in." Yeah, refereeing the two halves of himself. He couldn't decide if he was an idiot for messing things up with Elly or if the anger he felt at her attack was more than justified. Maybe a bit of both.

"That's okay. Delia has been a sweetheart and kept me company."

Will hazarded a glance back at Delia, who was

looking at him with a million and one questions in her eyes.

"She said a good friend took these amazing photographs." Kate walked across the office and touched the edge of the frame around one of Elly's scenes. The herd of elk depicted in it looked as if they might walk out of the foggy river valley where they were grazing right into his office.

"Yeah, Elly's very talented."

"Is her work sold here in town anywhere?"

Will wanted to say, "No." Something deep inside him didn't want Kate's and Elly's worlds to touch each other. But that was silly. If Kate bought some of Elly's photographs, maybe she would display them in her office back in Denver. Perhaps clients would see them and buy some of their own. Elly was talented, and more people should see that, despite his conflicted feelings toward her.

"There's a gallery down the street."

"Great, let's go." Kate hurried past him. "It was wonderful to meet you, Delia."

"Yeah. You, too."

Kate probably wouldn't be able to tell Delia wasn't being totally truthful. What had Kate said before he'd arrived?

When he looked at Delia, he tried to convey his surprise at Kate's appearance and that there was nothing for her to worry about, nothing that she should share with anyone. He wasn't sure she saw what he wanted her to, but he'd have to deal with that later.

Once he stepped out onto the front walk, Kate slipped her arm through his. As they walked toward downtown, she took in everything around them. "I can't believe I've never been here before. It's an adorable little town."

"I like it."

"So my being impulsive and showing up on your doorstep won't convince you to come back to the big city?"

"I'm sorry if that's why you came here."

"Only partly. Intense curiosity was the other. I had to see what took you away." She didn't say it as if she were angry or as if she'd been sitting at home pining away for him. That wasn't Kate's way.

He nodded toward the line of stores and the comings and goings of Cody's residents. "Now you see it."

They approached the Tangled Antlers Gallery, but when Will reached to open the door it flew open. Elly froze when she saw him. When she noticed Kate, he saw confusion and hurt in her eyes.

"Elly," he said, needing to say her name out loud, to draw her attention from Kate.

"Elly?" Kate asked. "Oh, this is the photographer. How fortunate you're here. Will was bringing me to see more of your wonderful work."

"Oh."

The awkwardness of the moment pressed in on Will. "Elly, this is Kate Sturgeon. We went to law school together." *Please, Kate, don't say anything else.*

"Nice to meet you," Elly said, but he could tell she didn't really mean it. She didn't offer to shake hands.

"You, too." Kate casually took a step to the side, moving herself farther away from him. "I was passing through the area and stopped to see what Will's raved about all these years, why he came back here instead of taking my father up on his offer to join our firm. I can certainly see why he made the choice. It's lovely here."

Kate met his eyes for a moment, her keen ones having missed nothing of what was really going on.

"I hope you enjoy your stay," Elly said. "I'm sorry, but I have to run."

Will ached as he watched her walk away, but he didn't want to chance a scene on the street, where everyone in the county would know about it before the end of the day. She didn't deserve that, not with everything else she was going through. Not even the cruel words she'd hurled at him could make him petty enough to deliberately hurt her.

"She's the reason you came back." Kate didn't sound hurt, perhaps more resigned.

He nodded. "I didn't know it at the time."

"You knew."

Maybe he had. Maybe he just hadn't admitted it in case a relationship with Elly never became reality.

"She's beautiful," Kate said. "I hope you work out whatever is going on between you."

"Me, too." His heart had never felt heavier.

"I have a feeling you won't need it, but the door is always open."

He tore his gaze away from the empty sidewalk where

Elly had been moments ago. He knew from the tone of Kate's voice that she would be leaving Cody as soon as she collected her things.

"Thanks. It was good to see you."

"You, too." She looked at the town around her. "Especially here. You fit."

Just like she fit in Denver.

"I think I'll take a rain check on the gallery today," she said. "Maybe another time."

"Be careful on your way home, okay?"

"Of course." She smiled at him. "I'd give you a kiss goodbye, but I have the feeling that it would get back to Elly in about three seconds."

He smiled back at her. "I think you have small-town life figured out already."

She reached out and quickly squeezed his hand. "Good luck. Elly's a lucky woman."

As he watched her cross the street and head for the parking lot where she'd evidently left her car, he hoped Elly would eventually think the same thing.

ELLY COULDN'T BREATHE. Seeing Will with another woman had been the single most horrible feeling of her life. Was this all-consuming heartache how her mother felt?

She'd seen guilt in Will's eyes, but was it for what had already happened between them or for his being with Kate now? Kate, who looked like she had walked off the pages of a fashion magazine.

They'd known each other in Denver. Would he go

back there now? The thought brought tears to her eyes, more pain than she could handle. She leaned her head forward on her steering wheel and squeezed her eyes against the tears that wanted to fall.

She couldn't deal with this now. Too much else was jockeying for space in her worry column—the upcoming Thanksgiving holiday, which would no doubt be like sitting on a powder keg; the Denver rodeo after that; figuring out how Mark would fit into their family and how her brothers would react to that; facing the fact that she would have to speak to her father again at some point. Adding the situation with Will to the mix—it was just too much.

She started the truck's engine and pulled out of the parking lot, deliberately not looking at anything but the road in front of her. She feared seeing Will and Kate again and how it might cause her to lose her precarious grip on her emotions.

As she left Cody and headed toward Markton, she gradually relaxed as much as she was able and started compartmentalizing. The only way she was going to get through the next couple of weeks was to only think about one obstacle at a time. First up, Thanksgiving and trying to figure out how to ensure no blood was shed, and nothing so horrible was said that it could never be taken back.

Chapter Twelve

Even though things felt anything but normal, the normality of cooking for Thanksgiving filled the days leading up to the big family meal. And despite the tension hanging over the ranch like dense fog, Anne Cody had made it clear that everyone would be at the family Thanksgiving dinner. No exceptions. And everyone would be civil or answer to her.

Since their mother was the main aggrieved party in the current disaster, Elly had convinced Jesse to set aside his simmering anger for a day just so they could all get through the required dinner.

More than once, Elly opened her mouth to ask how her mom was doing, but she couldn't force the words out. Plus, as shameful as it made her feel, she didn't think she could handle her mother's heartache on top of her own. So she went through the motions, just as she suspected everyone else would.

As her family ate its way through the traditional meal, Elly couldn't imagine it being any more uncomfortable. It was the first time they'd all been together since the revelation of her father's affair.

Normally, there was laughter and teasing around the table during the holidays, talk of the rodeo season, plans for the ranch next year, good-natured bets about the day's football games. This year should be extra special with the addition of Paula and her son, Clay, Josie and her son, Matt, and Maryanne, but it wasn't.

Instead, the conversation revolved around "Please pass the potatoes" and "Would anyone like any pumpkin pie?" The tension would dull any knife that tried to cut it.

Elly looked at her father, at the man responsible for this ruined holiday, and was shocked to see he wasn't even eating. He just stared at the food on his plate. He looked pale beneath his perpetual tan, his downcast eyes so unlike him. For a moment, worry flamed to life within her. He wasn't the youngest of men anymore. Was the stress of this situation too much for him?

Well, he'd brought it on himself, hadn't he? And onto the rest of them.

The longer the meal lasted, the more Elly thought of everything that was wrong with the picture. Her family not speaking, the gaping emptiness next to her where she wished Will was sitting. A Cody who wasn't even invited, who instead was eating a more modest meal with his wife, sister and the mother who probably couldn't even remember the affair that produced him.

Elly suspected the residents of Casper could hear the enormous sigh of relief when the meal was finally over. Her brothers vacated the premises so fast they nearly left the scent of burned rubber in their wake.

Paula, Josie and Maryanne offered to help clean up, but Anne told them to go spend the rest of the day with their families.

Elly and her mom didn't speak as they carried the dirty dishes and leftovers into the kitchen.

While loading the dishwasher, Elly noticed her mother scraping perfectly good food into the trash. A knot of unease grew in her stomach as her mom reached for an untouched pumpkin pie.

"Mom, I'd like to take the dessert over to Janie and her family."

"I'm sure they've already eaten something," Anne said without making eye contact.

"Maybe, but it's a good gesture nonetheless." Elly fought the anxiety gnawing at her, wondered when her subconscious had decided to take these steps.

Anne took a deep breath then let it out slowly. "You're right." She gripped the edge of the island until her knuckles went white. "None of this is Mark's fault."

Elly's stomach continued to churn as she drove toward Janie's home. How would she feel when she met Mark's eyes and knew he was her brother? What would he say?

She tried to force her nerves to calm as she pulled into the driveway at Janie's and walked to the front door, plate in hand. Janie opened the door before Elly had a chance to knock.

"Hey," Janie said.

"Hey." She held up the pie. "Hungry?"

"You didn't have to do that."

But as Elly followed Janie inside, she didn't smell any scents of festive cooking. In fact, everything was deathly quiet.

"How's your mom?"

"We just got her to sleep." Janie sounded exhausted. "She's having a bad day."

"I'm sorry."

Janie shrugged. "Thanks for the pie. I haven't gotten around to eating anything beyond this morning's Pop-Tarts."

Elly's heart ached for Janie, and she wished she could do something, anything, to make it better, easier.

"I'd planned to have a nice meal made when Mark and Nicki got back from her dad's, but…" Janie's voice caught on what sounded like a sob.

Elly closed the gap between them and wrapped her arms around Janie. "I'm sorry."

Janie shook her head against Elly's shoulder. "It's not your fault. I just feel like my life is unraveling. Mom's worse every day, and I can't stop feeling like I'm losing Mark. He doesn't talk to me like he used to."

Elly ran her hand over Janie's hair. "He will." Even if she had to kick him in the behind to get him to. Sure, he was probably feeling like his world had turned upside down too and now had a wife to talk to, but he had to consider how this affected his sister. The one he'd grown up with. No matter the biology, Elly still didn't feel like his sister.

A moan and a crash from Abigail's bedroom sent

Janie hurrying in that direction. "Thanks for the pie. I'll talk to you tomorrow, okay?"

"Sure." Elly stood in the kitchen and listened as Janie tried to get her mom to calm down. Tears welled in her eyes as she looked at the old linoleum, the cabinets in need of a new coat of paint.

Like Jesse, Mark was close to earning a championship in bullriding, perhaps his last chance because of his age. He'd made enough through the years that, along with Janie's income from the Feed and Grain, they'd been able to take care of their mother. But how much more could they do, how much better could they live, what dreams could they both accomplish if they had more money? Cody money. And it wouldn't be the handouts they both loathed if it belonged to Mark by right.

Elly looked up as the back door opened. Nicki, Mark's wife, walked in.

"Oh, hey," Nicki said.

"Hi, Nicki."

"Where's Janie?"

"In Abigail's room."

Their eyes met, and the sadness Elly felt was reflected in the eyes of the woman who'd captured Mark's heart. Elly was suddenly very glad Mark had Nicki. If only Janie had someone, too.

"I better go see if I can help," Nicki said.

Elly noticed Mark standing by the back fence staring out across the distance in front of him. "Hey, Nicki?"

"Yeah?"

"Do you think it'd be okay if I went out and talked to Mark?"

Nicki glanced toward her husband through the window. "I think that'd be good."

Elly nodded and headed out the back door. But a thought brought her back to the table. She slid a piece of the pumpkin pie off its plate onto a saucer and added a fork on the side.

Even before she reached Mark, she saw how he slumped as if a nearly unbearable weight pressed down on him. As she stepped up beside him, she lifted the saucer and said simply, "Pie?"

He looked at her for a moment, almost as if he didn't recognize her, then eyed the pie. "You didn't make it, did you?"

"Ha ha."

"I'm still not over that whole chocolate pie fiasco."

"Dude, that was nearly twenty years ago. Move on." She smiled at the memory. At age seven, she'd been determined to try to make a pie like her mom did. Only problem was she'd put in salt instead of sugar. Unluckily for Mark and Janie, they'd been the first ones to try it.

They stood in awkward silence for several beats before he took a bite of the pie. "Good." He took a couple more bites before speaking again. "So, is this as odd for you as it is for me?"

"Yep. It feels weird not knowing what to say around you. I mean...I've always thought of you as another brother. It's just..."

"You never knew I really was."

"Exactly."

"I'm not trying to hurt your family."

"I know." She really did. Mark was a good guy. He had to be to live through his hard life and grow up to be the type of man who took care of his family no matter what.

"I've just…been trying to figure out what it all means, where I fit in," he said.

She nodded and picked at a splinter sticking up from the wooden fence, beyond which grazed the few horses owned by the Hansens. "Mark, you need to talk to Janie."

"I know."

"She thinks she's losing you."

He looked over at her. "That's silly."

"Think of it from her point of view. We all know your…dad was a hard man. I know Janie wished several times that anyone else in the world could be your dad, and now you've got that. You have a way out. She doesn't."

"I would never abandon her. Or Mom. I've told her that."

"Maybe she needs to hear it again."

He shifted his attention to the house as Janie came out and headed toward the barn. He watched her as if he hadn't seen her in days. And perhaps he really hadn't if he hadn't picked up on how scared she was of being left alone to deal with their mother's worsening condition.

Elly took a couple steps back from the fence. "Well, I'm going to go."

"Thank you," he said. "For everything. You've been a good friend—to both of us."

The talk with Mark should have made her feel better, but by the time Elly returned to the ranch a sense of melancholy shadowed her every move. Not wanting to face anyone quite yet, she walked along the fence line beyond the barns as darkness fell around her. After several minutes, she stopped and climbed up to sit atop the fence. She stared up into the wide, star-studded Wyoming sky and acknowledged the truth that she'd tried to ignore all day.

She missed Will.

Really, really missed him.

Chapter Thirteen

"Dinner was wonderful, Mom," Will said as he scraped what little was left on his plate into the garbage.

"Thank you. But I think I'm going to be eating turkey for a month."

"You shouldn't have cooked so much for just the three of us."

"It's the Food Network. I get to watching Paula Deen and the other chefs, and I come up with too many things I want to try."

"I'll make a note to cancel it from your cable package."

His mother swatted him with a towel. "Don't you dare."

"Well, since you asked so nicely."

"Maybe one of these years we'll have a nice full table."

He knew she wasn't talking about food. "Mom."

His mom stopped washing plates and faced him. "What happened with Elly? I heard you two were seeing each other, something I should have heard from you, I might add."

"I don't want to talk about it."

"But why did you break up? You're so gorgeous together. You'd have beautiful children."

Will placed his hands on his mother's shoulders and leaned forward to kiss her on the forehead. "Thanks again for dinner. I've got to go do some work."

"On Thanksgiving?"

"The law doesn't take a holiday." And evidently his desire to see Elly never did either.

He headed home but found himself driving past his place. The last thing he wanted to do tonight was go home to a house that now harbored memories of her. Instead, he kept driving and pulled into the parking area next to his office. Maybe he would work some, see if today was any different from all the others when work couldn't keep his thoughts from straying to the woman he'd loved and lost.

Will trudged through the quiet night, imagining all the families in the surrounding houses kicking back to watch football or movies after stuffing themselves on too much holiday fare. For a moment, he stopped in the shadow of his office and imagined himself, Elly and a bunch of little blond children who looked like Elly sitting around a table filled to bursting with a Thanksgiving meal.

For a while, he'd thought such a scenario could be possible. After years of daydreaming about being with her, having been with her and then losing her was even worse. At least before he hadn't truly known what he didn't have. Now he knew every scent, every taste, every touch he might never experience again.

With a sigh, he went inside, flipping on lights as he went. He sank behind his desk and stared at the papers covering it. Determined to focus on something besides speculation about what Elly was doing right that moment, if she might be regretting what she'd said to him, he opened a file on a new case and started reading. He made notes and a to-do list, looked up additional information online. But thoughts of Elly still tugged at him from the periphery of his mind.

How had her Thanksgiving gone? Had it been tense? Stressful? Had she spoken to her father yet, or was she still giving him a wide berth?

He eyed the phone, even placed his hand on it, but he was afraid to call her. The idea of her hanging up on him or not taking his call in the first place left him with an awful aching in his chest. The part of him that felt wronged urged him to wait until she came to him.

The sound of a key in the door lock grabbed his attention. He tensed until he saw Delia stroll in.

She stopped in his doorway and crossed her arms. "Do *not* tell me you're sitting in here working on Thanksgiving."

"Okay, I won't."

She strode forward, closed the file atop his desk and motioned for him to follow her. "Come on."

"I'm busy, Delia."

"No, you're not. You're sitting in here wishing you were with Elly."

He wanted to be mad at her but couldn't. After all, she was right. "Do you annoy everyone like you do me?"

"Nah. You're special."

He smiled despite his better judgment. It would only encourage her.

"See. Already I'm better company than these four walls."

"Why aren't you with your family?"

"Been there, done that. Plus, you've met my family, right? They make me seem meek and mild."

Will leaned back in his chair, not ready to concede quite yet. "So, what do you have in mind?"

"The Lodgepole Café and a mega cup of coffee."

He sat for a moment then decided the Lodgepole did sound better than hiding in his office.

"Fine. But no delving into my personal life."

"I make no promises," Delia said as she headed for the door.

Even though he knew what was in store for him in a booth at the Lodgepole, he followed her anyway. The being alone thing just wasn't working, especially not tonight.

And by the looks of how many people were at the open 24/7/365 Lodgepole Café, he wasn't the only one feeling that way.

Despite both having had big meals with their families, he and Delia each ordered slices of pie—chocolate for her, lemon for him. Once the slices of pie, along with their three inches of meringue, arrived with steaming cups of coffee, Delia didn't waste time getting right to the heart of things.

"So, why are you moping about Elly instead of doing something about it?"

"What am I supposed to do? She's made it clear she doesn't want to see me—on two occasions." He'd told Delia about running into Elly outside the gallery.

"And you just walked away without a fight?"

"I'm supposed to fight with Elly?"

"More like not take no for an answer."

"You women are so confusing. I thought you all didn't like that kind of brutish behavior."

"I'm not saying throw her over your shoulder and grunt all the way back to your cave. Just make it known that you're not getting set aside that easily. You love her, and that's that."

He choked on the coffee he was sipping.

"Why does the word *love* always cause guys to choke or spasm or run?"

He didn't answer.

"You do love her, don't you? Guys usually don't mope or care what a woman says about them unless they're in love and things aren't going well."

He sat staring at the bite of pie on the end of his fork. He'd always loved Elly, but was it even more now? Deeper? A man so in love with a woman he couldn't imagine living without her no matter what hurdles they had to get past?

"If you do, then convince her you're supposed to be

together. Go after her. Don't let that Cody armor stand in your way."

The longer he sat listening to the hum of conversations around him, to the clink of silverware, the more Delia's words sank into him. He wasn't the boy he used to be, so why was he stepping away so easily? Yes, he'd made a mistake, but he didn't think it was an unforgivable one. Neither were her words, which he knew she didn't really mean deep down. It wasn't worth throwing away whatever the future could have in store for them.

It was time Elly Cody realized that she wasn't going to find anyone better than him. No one would love her the way he did.

Will met Delia's eyes. "Thank you."

She smiled. "Thank me with a nice, fat Christmas bonus."

"I might be able to arrange that."

"And how about putting a nice guy like you under my Christmas tree? I promise, I've been very good this year."

Will laughed. "Sorry, you're on your own there."

Delia pouted. "Some girls have all the luck."

Will knew he'd be the lucky one if Elly and he could mend the rift between them and she took him back.

ELLY DECIDED NOT TO fly to Denver. The open road and uninterrupted hours to think sounded really appealing. But because she was driving, she had to hit the highway the morning after Thanksgiving—something she decided while sitting out beneath the stars the night before.

She hefted her saddle and placed it in its designated spot in the trailer. When she stepped back outside, her mother stood between her and the tack room in the barn.

"Mom."

"Good morning, dear. I hear you're driving to Denver."

Elly headed toward the barn. "Yeah. Feel like a good road trip."

"Mind some company?"

Yes, she minded. Still, she asked, "Who?"

"Me."

Elly stopped and stared at her mother. "You want to go to Denver?"

"Yes. Is that so surprising? After all, it's a big event for you and Jesse."

Elly didn't point out that her mother could much more easily ride on the plane with the rest of the family. Or that she didn't go to that many of the out-of-state rodeos anymore, preferring to stay at home and work with the mares. Something told her that her mother needed those miles of open road just as much as she did. That things remained strained at the main house. Perhaps her mom couldn't face being trapped with the tension that would no doubt permeate the plane.

Even though Elly really needed the alone time, she nodded. "Okay, but I'd planned to leave in a couple of hours."

"I'm already packed."

Elly laughed. "Confident of my answer, huh?"

"Seriously, would you say no to your mother?" A cheeky smile tugged at the edges of Anne's mouth.

"Not if I want to be kept in delicious, waist-obliterating desserts."

Anne rolled her eyes and headed back to her house to get her luggage.

The fact her mother had smiled for the first time in days lifted Elly's heart despite how much it still ached, wanting to be near Will again.

She wondered if that particular ache would ever go away.

She'd heard Kate had left town almost immediately after Elly had seen her with Will. She couldn't help wondering why. Or worrying that the longer she and Will didn't talk, the more likely it was that he'd go back to Denver.

But she didn't let herself call him. She needed him to be the one to come to her, to apologize, to convince her that it would never happen again. She needed to be able to believe him without a single doubt.

As she finished loading her gear and luggage and finally guided Pepper and Summer Gal, her backup horse, into the trailer, she tried not to focus on the fact that she was the one who'd pushed Will away. She didn't want to blame herself, not when he was the one who'd made a mistake.

Still, she couldn't stop the irrational hurt that he hadn't called, that he hadn't tried harder to win her back, that he hadn't raced out to the ranch insisting that they were meant for each other like some knight in shining armor.

Elly scoffed at the idea as she closed the trailer behind the horses. There were no knights in shining armor—especially not ones wearing business suits and keeping secrets.

WILL EASED OFF THE ACCELERATOR. He wouldn't be able to proclaim his love to Elly if he careened off a cliff into a ravine, would he? But it proved difficult not to speed up again. He'd already wasted too much time trying to figure out what he was going to say and how, and he still hadn't nailed down a plan. He'd fumble his way through it, if necessary.

But it all came down to three little words. Maybe he'd just utter those and take it from there.

The entrance road to the Cottonwood Ranch seemed to stretch twice as long as normal, torturing him. He fantasized about Elly running to him as soon as she saw him, like some cheesy ending to a chick flick. But he knew the likelihood of that scenario was next to nil. He would have to work much harder to win her back—and that was okay. She was worth it.

The reality was he parked, got out of his vehicle and didn't see her anywhere. Maybe she was out in the practice facility, but he decided to check the house first. When he knocked, it wasn't Elly who opened the door. Instead, Jesse stared out at him as if he couldn't com-

prehend why Will was there—at least at first. A switch
seemed to flip on inside him, signaling recognition.

"Elly isn't here."

"When will she be back?"

"She's on her way to Denver."

"Already?"

"She drove this time." Jesse eyed him as if he might
be considering drawing and quartering. "What happened
with you two?"

"That's between us."

Will wondered if the thought of beating the information out of him entered Jesse's mind. It if did, it didn't
stay long because Jesse stepped back and motioned Will
inside. "Want some coffee?"

The last thing he needed was something to jack up
his anxiety even more, but being on big brother's good
side wasn't a bad idea. So, instead of chasing after Elly
as he wanted to, he followed Jesse inside.

"I shouldn't have brought you into this," Jesse said.

Will's muscles tightened, ready to go toe-to-toe with
the other man, to tell him he was worthy of Elly even if
he didn't come from money or ride the rodeo circuit.

"I should have gotten someone we didn't know, someone it wouldn't have mattered if Elly hated when he
brought the proof of our father's adultery."

Elly hated him? His heart weighed heavy as a cold
stone in his chest.

Damn, he should have stayed in Colorado. At least
then, the loss of her was that of a first crush and had
dimmed with time.

Now? It was like someone was using a carving knife on his insides.

It took Will a moment to realize Jesse was holding a cup of coffee out to him. He took the steaming cup but didn't raise it to his lips.

"Whatever happened, Elly hasn't been happy the past few days. I don't pretend to know how women's minds work, but I think she misses you."

Hope flared in Will. Maybe he hadn't ruined his only chance. Maybe she had lashed out only because she was hurting so much. He met Jesse's gaze. "I love your sister."

Jesse nodded. "I expected as much. But I'm not the one you need to tell. If she makes the Finals, she'll start for Vegas immediately. It'll be a couple of weeks at least before she's home."

An idea began forming in Will's mind. He placed his untouched coffee on the kitchen table. "I don't think I can wait that long." He headed toward the door, making plans with each step.

"Will."

He stopped and looked back at Jesse.

"She's not too happy with men in general right now."

"I can be persuasive." He'd waited a long time for Elly, even when he hadn't realized that was what he was doing. He didn't intend to wait any longer. And unlike his younger self, he wasn't going to sit meekly by. This time, he'd fight for what he wanted—and convince Elly it was what she wanted, too.

Nothing—not his age, not her family, not her efforts to protect herself by pushing him away, not his stupid mistake—was going to stand in his way.

Chapter Fourteen

Elly stared at the rugged mountains of the Wyoming landscape as her truck ate up the miles between Markton and Denver. The angle of the setting sun cast a lovely orange glow over the Rockies.

Her mom, who had been reading in silence for the past couple of hours, closed the book and rubbed her eyes.

"Must be a good book. You looked absorbed."

"Nothing like a good book."

"To take your mind off real life?" Elly probably shouldn't have said anything, but the not talking was getting to her.

"Sometimes."

Elly returned her attention to the highway. "How can you stand it?"

"I still love your father, honey. Despite the problems years ago, we have a good marriage."

"Years ago? What about the problems now?"

"They're the same ones. Just old wounds reopened."

Elly glanced at her mother. "You knew about the affair when it happened?"

Anne sat without speaking for a few seconds. "Soon after."

"And you stayed with him?"

"Yes. I loved him, and he loved me."

Elly shook her head. "Men who cheat on their wives don't love them." The words tasted bitter coming out—and like a lie. She'd seen her parents together through the years. Could her father fake love that well?

"People make mistakes," Anne said.

"Don't I know it."

Her mother shifted in her seat, facing Elly more fully. "This about your father or Will?"

"Dad."

"You sure about that?"

Elly tried to speak, but the words died in her throat.

"What happened?"

Elly listened to the truck's wheels singing against the pavement. "It doesn't matter. It's over."

"Yeah, I can tell by the way you've said about ten words since we left the ranch. The way your heartache has been riding along with us like another passenger."

"I'm fine. It's you I'm worried about."

"I'll be okay."

"Mom, don't try to fool me. I've seen how upset you've been. I saw you crying."

"You want to know why I was crying?"

"I already know. It's obvious."

"You only think you know. Honey, your father and I both did things we're ashamed of now. We were young and selfish. And now they're coming back and hurting everyone we love. And that's what is making me sad—how this is affecting you and your brothers. Janie. Mark. You all are the innocent bystanders of bad decisions."

Elly sensed there was more to the story of what happened all those years ago, but she honestly didn't want to know any more. She'd had enough disillusionment.

Another mile ticked by on the odometer before Anne spoke again. "Why did you and Will break up?"

Elly shrugged. "It just wasn't working out."

"Why?" Anne Cody did not give up easily.

"We're too different."

"I got the feeling that's why you liked him—because he's not like the other guys you've dated."

"For a bit. But rodeo is my life."

"It's part of your life. You're also a talented photographer, a wonderful face to the ranch." Anne paused. "A beautiful young woman who deserves to be loved by a man."

"Will doesn't love me."

"Did he say that?"

"No."

"Then what makes you say it?"

"He lied to me, okay? Just like all men lie." Elly choked on the last word and turned to stare out her side window for a moment before returning her attention to the highway ahead of them.

"What did he lie about?"

Maybe if she told her mom, all the questions would

stop. All the questions that hurt because, despite everything, she missed Will horribly.

"He knew about the results of the paternity test and didn't tell me."

"Ah. So he didn't actually lie."

"Omission is just as bad."

"Elly, don't let what happened with your father color your view of all men. Will is kind, hardworking, smart, not to mention very handsome."

"I know all that," Elly whispered, her anger at Will dissolving more by the second. "But how can I trust him?"

"Ask yourself why he didn't tell you."

She went with the safer of the two answers. "Because Jesse was the one who hired him, not me."

"Is that what he said?"

Elly nodded.

"I think it's more than that."

Yeah, he knew he wouldn't get what he wanted. But she couldn't tell her mother that.

The thought ate at Elly as she let it sit there in her brain unspoken. If she set aside her hurt, she knew the accusation felt wrong, unfair.

"I think Will knew how you'd react and couldn't face it," Anne said. "That boy has been in love with you since before his voice changed."

Elly lifted her right hand from the steering wheel. "Am I the only person who didn't know this? God, how self-centered have I been my whole life?"

"Not self-centered. Driven."

"I feel like the world's most clueless person."

Her mother smiled. "Better late than never."

"That I feel clueless?"

"That you find love. You do love him, don't you?"

Elly exhaled slowly. "Yes."

"You don't sound happy about it."

"I've ruined it. I said some things. Not nice things."

"That's what apologies are for, honey."

As the sun disappeared below the mountains, taking the orange glow with it, Elly tried to imagine how she could apologize for comparing Will to an adulterer. Did she want to take a chance with Will?

Yes. Her gut—her heart—told her Will wasn't like her father.

But she couldn't help wondering if she was just being as blind as her mother had been.

"Do you think Walker and Paula will make it?" Anne asked, surprising Elly with the change in topic.

"Of course. They're crazy in love."

Her mom nodded, looking as if she was considering the validity of that argument. "What about Dex and Josie?"

"Yes."

"Dusty and Maryanne?" Anne was halfway through asking the last question when it hit Elly what her mother was doing. "Every couple is different. They have their own problems, their own ways of getting through them and making up." Anne lifted the romance novel. "Their own paths to happily ever after."

Elly watched as her mom opened the book and began

reading where she'd left off. If her mom still believed in love conquering all, why couldn't she?"

WILL PULLED BACK ONTO THE highway after receiving his much-deserved speeding ticket. He didn't care how many he got on his way to Colorado as long as he caught Elly and made her believe they belonged together.

When the Wyoming Highway Patrol officer passed Will's SUV and sped away, Will glanced at his cell phone to see if he had service yet. When he saw he did, he called Delia at home.

"If you're calling to tell me to come to work, I quit."

He smiled. "No, actually, I might not be in for a few days."

A tractor-trailer rig passed him, the sound of the big engine blocking out Delia's response. "What?"

"Where are you?"

"Between Casper and Cheyenne."

"You're working again today?"

"No. You'd be proud. I'm doing something romantic."

"Oh? Can't wait to hear this."

"Prepare to eat that sarcasm." He paused, an unexpected wave of nervousness washing over him.

"Well, don't keep me in suspense, Prince Charming."

"I'm going to Colorado—after Elly."

"Oh, Will." All hint of teasing was gone from Delia's voice. "I'm so glad."

"Wish me luck."

"You're not going to need it. But I fully expect you two to name one of your children after me."

Will laughed before hanging up. As he drove along the same roads Elly had traveled only hours earlier, he couldn't stop smiling. He hoped Delia was right—that Elly loved him enough that he wouldn't have to depend on luck.

ELLY PULLED INTO A GAS station south of Cheyenne. After setting the gas to pumping, she tapped the truck's passenger side window. "You need to go inside?"

"You go first. I'll watch the pump."

Elly wandered into the convenience store to visit the ladies' room then pick up some candy and soda. As she reached the end of the candy bar aisle, she spotted a teenage couple giving each other googly eyes in front of a display of snack cakes. The picture of young love made her heart contract.

How she wished Will were here now. She'd done a lot of thinking since her conversation with her mom earlier. When she got home, she was going to make things right, tell Will that as crazy at it sounded, she didn't want to be with anybody else—ever.

She yearned to call him, tell him now. But she wanted to see the look in his brown eyes when she said the words, be able to feel him immediately take her in his arms if he felt the same way.

Elly paid for her purchases and headed back to the truck in time to see her mom end a call on her cell phone and hop out of the truck to remove the fuel nozzle from the truck's tank.

"Who were you talking to?"

"Nobody. Wrong number."

Elly stared at her mom because her words didn't have the ring of truth. Maybe she'd been talking to Elly's dad and just didn't want to get into another disagreement about that relationship.

When they pulled back onto the highway, Elly's thoughts wouldn't veer away from her father.

"How did you do it?" Elly wasn't sure she'd meant to verbalize the words, but they tumbled out anyway.

"What, dear?"

"Stay with Dad, knowing he'd had an affair? Did you know it was Abigail?"

"Yes, I knew."

Elly gripped the steering wheel more tightly. "I couldn't have handled that."

Her mother sighed and clasped her hands together in her lap. "It was hard, but it wasn't long before I got pregnant with Jesse. And then the rest of you came along, and things gradually got better."

"But you'd still see her all the time."

"She didn't know."

"What?"

"Abigail didn't know your father was married when… they were together. She wasn't from here. But she broke it off as soon as she found out."

"But Dad did know."

"I'm not excusing what he did. I'm just saying it was

a difficult time. I wasn't in a good place after...I lost our first child. Honestly, I teetered on the edge for a while."

"But he should have been there supporting you, not..." Elly couldn't bring herself to voice the rest of the thought.

"Yes. But it's in the past now. We worked through it because we decided there was more positive about our marriage than negative. It was worth saving. Sometimes people do things when they're under stress that they wouldn't normally do. It doesn't mean they don't regret it and wish with all their heart they could take it back later on."

Elly glanced at her mom. The feeling she'd had earlier—that there was more meaning behind her mother's words—tugged at her again. But some sense she couldn't explain told her not to dig that deep.

"I know it may take some time," Anne said, "but I hope you'll find it in your heart to forgive your father. He really does love you and your brothers more than life itself."

"What about Mark?"

"He doesn't know him as well. But it'll come with time."

A horrible thought made Elly's hands tighten on the steering wheel. "Did Dad know about Mark all these years?"

At first, Elly didn't think her mother was going to answer.

"Not for sure."

"But he knew the possibility was there?"

"Yes. But so did I."

"How—"

"Leave it, Elly." Anne's tone—one part stern parent, one part plea—left no room for argument.

A million questions swirled in Elly's mind, begging her to ask them. Instead, she stared into the night and tried to figure out what might have happened back then. Why her mother, for some reason, at least partially blamed herself.

ELLY WALKED AROUND THE EDGE of the arena, headed for the bleachers so she could watch Jesse's practice ride. She and Pepper had already gone through their practice runs, and she was fighting an apathy she'd never known. She still wanted the title, but with everything that was going on in her life the Finals just paled in comparison. She hated that the situation with her family and the fight with Will were jeopardizing her dream, but how was she supposed to turn off those thoughts long enough to ride, and ride well?

When she looked up, a familiar figure stood at the edge of the arena, her left boot and both forearms propped up on the fence.

"Janie?"

Janie turned around and smiled. "Hey."

Elly rushed forward and hugged her. "What are you doing here?"

"I rode down with Nicki and Mark."

"Oh." Elly hated the awkwardness that descended

at the mention of his name. The brother they now shared.

Elly thought about Abigail and found she didn't hate her. By her mother's account, Abigail hadn't knowingly done anything wrong. She'd still been single and had no idea Elly's father wasn't. And Elly found it impossible to harbor ill will toward a woman who didn't even have full control of her mind anymore.

"Who's with your mom?"

Janie looked startled that Elly would even bring up her mother, now that the truth was out there. "Uh, Ruth is staying with her. Mom's on a new medication, and it seems to be helping some."

"Good." She meant it. Elly couldn't imagine how horrible it must be to feel one's thoughts and memories slipping away as if they were being erased and leaving a blank page behind.

"Mark's up," Janie said and focused on the chute where Mark situated himself atop a red bull named Spitfire.

Elly held her breath alongside Janie as Mark nodded that he was ready. Of course, she'd be rooting for Jesse, but she found she wanted Mark to do well, too. Do well and not get hurt. She gripped the fence as the gate swung open and the bull started bucking.

Elly couldn't take her eyes off Mark, willing him to have a safe ride. Trying to recast him in her mind as her brother. She found it wasn't too much of a leap from how she'd always thought of him.

The buzzer sounded at eight seconds and Mark made a safe dismount.

"That would get a good score," Elly said. She glanced over to see Janie beaming with pride.

"I hope so."

Elly heard the hopes and dreams of the entire Hansen family in those three little words. Shame that she'd always had things so easy, that she'd been moping about her own problems when she had so much going for her, had her stepping back. "You want a Coke?"

Janie glanced at her, confusion in her eyes. "Jesse's up next."

"I'll be back in time. He takes forever and a day in the chute."

"Okay, sure."

Elly headed for the concession area, needing a few moments alone. She tried to picture the months ahead, how Mark would fit into her family, how much he might want to—or not. When she really thought about it, she could picture everyone eventually coming to a sort of peace with the situation, accepting Mark and what had happened.

Except maybe Jesse. Even before the paternity issue, those two had a simmering animosity toward each other. Sure, she'd thought it might be lessening after the Oklahoma City Rodeo, but that was before sibling rivalry had been added to the mix.

Elly shook her head as she turned back toward the arena with two drinks. She needed to just let it go, let

Jesse and Mark deal with their own issues. She had plenty of her own.

As she approached Janie, her friend didn't notice her. Something about the look on Janie's face caused Elly to stop and stare. It looked like…longing.

Elly redirected her attention to where Janie was staring so intently, and it landed on Jesse. She glanced back at Janie and felt as if she'd taken a jolt from a cattle prod. How long had this been going on? On their getaway weekend, had Jesse been the one Janie was thinking about? Why hadn't she told Elly?

Was this something else that had existed right in front of her nose for a long time without her realizing it?

Elly's heart broke a little. Did Janie think she didn't have a chance with Jesse because of who she was? Because of his long-standing rivalry with Mark? After all the recent revelations, did she feel the possibility was even more remote?

Jesse came out of the gate riding a huge gray bull. But Elly kept her eyes on Janie, watching as tension radiated from her like summer heat off the highway. How torn up must Janie be inside to want her brother to do well but also the man who was his chief rival—the man she so obviously cared about?

The bull tossed Jesse after only about five seconds, and he quickly rolled out of the way of those dangerous hooves. He jumped to his feet, not looking the least bit happy.

The tension flowed out of Janie as she dropped back

off her toes and turned toward Elly. She froze, her eyes widening as she realized Elly had seen everything.

Not wanting to cause Janie any further anxiety, she smiled and walked forward, extending the soda. "I think I'll steer clear of him for the next few minutes. I'm sure what he's saying would light my hair on fire."

Janie relaxed a little and took the cold drink. "Tough bull. Hasn't been ridden but half a dozen times this year."

They fell into random rodeo chitchat for the next couple of minutes until Janie's furtive glances toward the end of the arena got the better of Elly. Being around someone so obviously pining for someone else reminded her of Will and how much she missed him. Suddenly, she wanted nothing more than to be alone.

"I'll catch you later. I'm going to go back and rest a bit before tonight."

"Oh, okay."

Elly hurried from the arena, and drove back to her hotel room before the first tears fell. She curled onto her side on the bed and let out all the emotions bottled up inside her. Things were coming from all sides, but the one that hit her hardest was that moment when she'd yelled at Will, accused him of something so awful that she wouldn't blame him for not speaking to her again.

But she couldn't accept that—not without trying to fix what she'd messed up.

She sat on the side of the bed and dialed his house number. It rang several times before his voice mail kicked on. She listened to his voice, pressing the phone closer to her ear so she could feel as if he was there with her.

She didn't leave a message, but rather hung up and dialed his cell, suddenly desperate to reach him. As it rang on the other end, she heard someone's phone ring outside her room. When it happened a second time and then a third, she stared at the door, almost afraid to hope.

Her breathing accelerated as she walked toward the door, the phone still pressed to her ear. The call went to Will's voice mail just as she opened the door and saw him standing there.

"Will." She was afraid to blink, afraid he'd be gone when she opened her eyes again.

When he smiled, she launched herself at him. He laughed as she careened into him, knocking him back a couple of steps. And then he was kissing her, pulling her to him and backing her into the room, kicking the door closed behind him.

"I'm so sorry," she managed to say between kisses.

"You should be. I'm sorry, too."

"I was so awful. I didn't mean those things I said."

He stepped back and framed her face with his hands. "I know."

"Why aren't you madder?" She tried to pull away, but he wouldn't let her.

"I was, for a while. Yes, I made a mistake, but I didn't deserve some of the things you said."

"I know. You should hate me."

"Would that make you feel better?"

"Yes. No." She shook her head. "I don't know."

"You know what I think?"

She looked up at him, love welling inside her. "No."

"I think that you were upset. You were right. I shouldn't have let things progress like they did without telling you about Mark, at least waiting until I'd told Jesse and you'd found out from him."

"Why didn't you?"

He ran the back of his fingers along her jaw. "Because I wanted you so much. Because when I'm around you, I can't think straight." He smiled. "You've always had that effect on me."

"Always?"

"Elly Cody, I've loved you for so long I can't remember a time when I didn't."

She lowered her eyes. "And I was too caught up in myself to notice."

He lifted her chin, forcing her to look into his eyes. "Stop. It wasn't the right time. We both had to go be the people we were going to be first."

Elly laughed. "But I'm no different."

"That's where you're wrong."

"How am I different? I'm still at the ranch, still working for my family, still chasing after this racing dream."

"You don't see yourself as I do. You were always beautiful, especially to me, but now you're a grown woman, confident, talented. You never gave up on your dream, but you've got this entire new side to yourself.

The artist, the woman who is going to travel the world and make her mark on it."

Elly's heart filled with love for this man when he said those words, like he would never doubt her, no matter what she wanted to do.

"You're amazing," she said.

"I'm just a guy telling the truth."

"Will you go with me?"

"Go where?"

"Around the world? I don't want to see it alone."

He gifted her with one of his beautiful smiles. She'd never tire of them.

"Ellen Cody, I'd follow you anywhere."

"Anywhere?" she asked as she took his hand and started walking backward.

He eyed the bed then met her eyes. "Anywhere," he said, his voice deep and sexy and full of promise.

Chapter Fifteen

Elly checked Pepper's saddle, making sure it was adjusted correctly. Movement several feet away caught her attention. When she looked over Pepper's back, she saw her father standing there. Shock registered right before the desire to look anywhere but at him. For the first time in her life, she had no idea what to say to her father. And for the first time, he looked to be at a loss for words, too.

As he took a few steps forward, Elly stood rooted. J.W. lifted his work-roughened hand and scratched between Pepper's ears. "I can remember the first time you sat on a horse like it was yesterday, the excitement on your face when you first raced."

Words still didn't come to Elly, stuck somewhere in her brain where she couldn't reach them.

"I know you've been angry lately, and rightly so." He met Elly's eyes then and held her gaze. "But whatever you're feeling about me, set it aside for tonight. You've worked too long and hard to let my mistake rob you of your dream."

Why had he come here like this? She'd been doing fine. She'd had good times in her practices, was in the hunt because of her hard work all year. And she was excited that somewhere out in those stands of spectators sat Will, cheering her on.

She and her father stood staring at each other for several interminable seconds before he gave a single nod. "Good luck." When he turned away, something about the lines in his profile and the less-than-erect posture hit her like a kick from a horse. He looked so much older than he had weeks ago. It shocked her because J. W. Cody had always been bigger than life, robust, able to take on anything the world threw at him.

Except maybe the repercussions of his own mistakes.

In that moment, she saw a flash of Abigail Hansen, of the confused shell of her former self she'd become. What if something happened to her father and she'd never forgiven him? Would she ever be able to forgive herself?

Things with Will were going well, and she was one event away from making the Finals. She wanted to be fully happy again, to not be estranged from her family.

"Dad."

He stopped and turned slowly back toward her, like he didn't trust that he'd actually heard her speak.

"Thanks." It wasn't much, but it was a start.

And it seemed to be enough for her dad. He offered her a smile, then walked away.

It was as if their conversation had pushed all other sound away, but it came rushing back in time for her to realize it was almost time to ride. She mounted Pepper and prepared to chase the dream around those oh-so-familiar barrels.

Part of her fate rested on her performance, but another part depended on the rides of three other racers who were close to her in the standings. Her anxiety built as she had to watch the other three go before her, all clocking good times.

She stroked Pepper's neck and leaned close to the mare's right ear. "It's all up to us, girl."

Elly moved into position, but it wasn't the regular voice of announcer Rusty Thornhugh that came over the public address speakers. It was Will's.

"Next up is Elly Cody, one hell of a barrel racer—and the woman I love."

Rumbles went through the crowd, but Elly couldn't take her eyes off Will where he stood in the announcer's booth wearing a red, western-style shirt that made her smile. He met her gaze.

"Elly, I've loved you for what seems like forever, but never more than I do at this moment. That's why I'm asking you to marry me."

Elly gasped and tears threatened. She lifted her hand to her mouth in disbelief. She saw him smile.

"You've got the length of your ride to think about it. And you better ride like the wind because I've got a hankering to see Vegas."

Though she didn't want to stop looking at him, she had a ride to get through—and she planned to have the race of her life.

She shut out the sounds around her and focused on the course ahead. Pepper seemed to be reading her mind because she bolted forward like a bullet. They rounded the first barrel at a screaming pace. Elly's heart hammered as she urged Pepper toward barrel number two. They came so close to it, she'd swear they left skid marks on its side.

Elly eyed the third barrel and felt the wind race by her as Pepper flew toward the final turn. When they rounded it safely, Elly nearly screamed in triumph. Instead, she lowered her body and urged Pepper toward home. She held her breath as she crossed the finish.

The roar of applause filled the arena when her time showed she'd beaten the next highest score by a full second—a blowout by barrel-racing standards. She leaned forward and hugged Pepper. "We did it, girl."

"Whooee, let's rename that horse Lightning. That's a winning time, ladies and gentlemen," Rusty announced as Elly slid off Pepper's back and spotted Will, standing at the edge of the arena.

Elly ran toward him as fast as her trembling legs would carry her. When she reached him, she leaped onto the fence in front of him. "Yes," she said just before she pulled his lips down to hers.

"That looks like a yes to me, folks," Rusty said over the speakers. "And I hear they have wedding chapels in Vegas."

* * * * *

We hope you're enjoying the Cody family saga!
Watch for the other stories featuring these
men and women of the West:

WALKER: THE RODEO LEGEND (June 2010)
DEXTER: HONORABLE COWBOY (July 2010)
DUSTY: WILD COWBOY (August 2010)
MARK: SECRET COWBOY (September 2010)

And be sure to look for the series finale next month!
JESSE: MERRY CHRISTMAS, COWBOY
(November 2010)
Available wherever Harlequin books are sold.

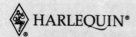

HARLEQUIN®

American ★ Romance®

COMING NEXT MONTH

Available November 9, 2010

#1329 THE SHERIFF'S CHRISTMAS SURPRISE
Babies & Bachelors USA
Marie Ferrarella

#1330 JESSE: MERRY CHRISTMAS, COWBOY
The Codys: The First Family of Rodeo
Lynnette Kent

#1331 SANTA IN A STETSON
Fatherhood
Rebecca Winters

#1332 MIRACLE BABY
Baby To Be
Laura Bradford

REQUEST YOUR FREE BOOKS!
2 FREE NOVELS PLUS 2 FREE GIFTS!

HARLEQUIN®

American ★ Romance®

Love, Home & Happiness!

YES! Please send me 2 FREE Harlequin® American Romance® novels and my 2 FREE gifts (gifts are worth about $10). After receiving them, if I don't wish to receive any more books, I can return the shipping statement marked "cancel." If I don't cancel, I will receive 4 brand-new novels every month and be billed just $4.24 per book in the U.S. or $4.99 per book in Canada. That's a saving of at least 15% off the cover price! It's quite a bargain! Shipping and handling is just 50¢ per book.* I understand that accepting the 2 free books and gifts places me under no obligation to buy anything. I can always return a shipment and cancel at any time. Even if I never buy another book from Harlequin, the two free books and gifts are mine to keep forever.

154/354 HDN E5LG

Name _____ (PLEASE PRINT) _____

Address _____ Apt. # _____

City _____ State/Prov. _____ Zip/Postal Code _____

Signature (if under 18, a parent or guardian must sign)

Mail to the Harlequin Reader Service:
IN U.S.A.: P.O. Box 1867, Buffalo, NY 14240-1867
IN CANADA: P.O. Box 609, Fort Erie, Ontario L2A 5X3

Not valid for current subscribers to Harlequin® American Romance® books.

Want to try two free books from another line?
Call 1-800-873-8635 or visit www.morefreebooks.com.

* Terms and prices subject to change without notice. Prices do not include applicable taxes. N.Y. residents add applicable sales tax. Canadian residents will be charged applicable provincial taxes and GST. Offer not valid in Quebec. This offer is limited to one order per household. All orders subject to approval. Credit or debit balances in a customer's account(s) may be offset by any other outstanding balance owed by or to the customer. Please allow 4 to 6 weeks for delivery. Offer available while quantities last.

Your Privacy: Harlequin is committed to protecting your privacy. Our Privacy Policy is available online at www.eHarlequin.com or upon request from the Reader Service. From time to time we make our lists of customers available to reputable third parties who may have a product or service of interest to you. If you would prefer we not share your name and address, please check here. ☐

Help us get it right—We strive for accurate, respectful and relevant communications. To clarify or modify your communication preferences, visit us at www.ReaderService.com/consumerschoice.

HARI0R

HARLEQUIN®

A Romance

FOR EVERY MOOD™

Spotlight on

Inspirational

Wholesome romances
that touch the heart and soul.

See the next page
to enjoy a sneak peek from
the Love Inspired® Suspense
inspirational series.

*The mission trip to Mexico was supposed to be an
adventure. But the thrill turns sour when Jenna Dougherty
and her roommate Magdalena are kidnapped.*

"It's okay. I'm here to help." The voice was as deep as the darkness, but Jenna Dougherty didn't believe the lie. She could do nothing but lie still as hands slid down her arms, felt the rope around her wrists.

"I'm going to use a knife to cut you free, Jenna. Hold still."

The cold blade of a knife pressed close to her head before her gag fell away.

"I—" she started, but her mouth was dry, and she could do nothing but suck in air.

"Shhh. Whatever needs to be said can be said when we're out of here." Nick spoke quietly, his hand gentle on her cheek. There and gone as he sliced through the ropes on her wrists and ankles.

He pulled her upright. "Come on. We may be on borrowed time."

"I can't leave my friend," Jenna rasped out.

"There's no one here. Just us."

"She has to be here." Jenna took a step away.

"There's no one here. Let's go before that changes."

"It's dark. Maybe if we find a light…"

"What did you say?"

"We need to turn on the light. I can't leave until I know that—"

"What can you see, Jenna?"

"Nothing."

"No shadows? No light?"

"No."

"It's broad daylight. There's light spilling in from the window I climbed in through. You can't see it?"

She went cold at his words.

"I can't see anything."

"You've got a nasty bruise on your forehead. Maybe that has something to do with it." His fingers traced the tender flesh on her forehead.

"It doesn't matter *how* it happened. I'm blind!"

Can Nick help Jenna find her friend or will chasing this trail have Jenna running blindly again into danger?

Find out in RUNNING BLIND, available in November 2010 only from Love Inspired Suspense.

SHLISEXP1110

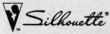
Silhouette®

ROMANTIC
SUSPENSE
Sparked by Danger, Fueled by Passion.

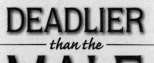
DEADLIER
than the
MALE

BY *NEW YORK TIMES* AND
USA TODAY BESTSELLING AUTHOR

SHARON
SALA
AND
COLLEEN THOMPSON

Women can be dangerous enemies
but love will conquer all.

Available November wherever books are sold.